Unbound Publishing

Presents

Brokered Submission

CLAIRE THOMPSON

EDITED BY
DONNA FISK
JAE ASHLEY

COVER ART - KELLY SHORTEN

FINE LINE EDIT - KATHY KOZAKEWICH

PRINT ISBN 978-1505455960

COPYRIGHT 2014 CLAIRE THOMPSON

COPYRIGHT - COVER ART IMAGE

MYSTOCK88PHOTO | DREAMSTIME.COM

ALL RIGHTS RESERVED

Chapter 1

"That's it for me." Ed slid out of the booth and stood. "My dad's expecting me." He glanced down at Dylan. "You need a ride back to the office?"

Dylan barely glanced at his business partner before returning his gaze to Zoë. "No thanks. I'm good. Have a good night, Ed. Say hi to your dad for me."

Zoë's boss, Bob Siegel, also hoisted himself out of the booth. "I better get going too. My wife already texted three times." He grinned down at Zoë. "How about you? Need a ride to the subway?"

The four of them were celebrating the completion of a lucrative financial deal put together by their two firms. In the two weeks they'd worked together, Dylan Hart had been all business, but something was different tonight. Though the two older men seemed unaware, there was a definite sexual undercurrent going on between Dylan and Zoë since they'd arrived at the trendy downtown bar earlier that evening. Until tonight, Zoë hadn't permitted herself to think of the admittedly attractive man as anything but a colleague, but now the flirtatious subtext between them, combined with the buzz from her drink, had left her feeling a little reckless.

Dylan was staring at her with those intense golden-brown eyes, one eyebrow cocked, something in his face saying, *Stay. I dare you.* Zoë's heart began to race, her nipples tingling, the hairs rising along the back of her neck. She wanted to look away from his mesmerizing gaze, but was unable to do so. Without looking at Bob, she found herself replying, "No thanks. I think I'll stay for one more drink."

After Zoë's boss and Dylan's partner had gone, they moved together to the bar to order another drink, settling side-by-side on swiveling stools. They talked easily for a while about various business ventures, rumors of takeovers and potential opportunities. In between, they managed to establish that neither of them was currently involved. Though the banter remained easy, if anything, the sexual undercurrent intensified.

Earlier in the evening, Dylan had loosened his collar and tie and unbuttoned the top buttons of his shirt. Zoë found herself staring at his throat as he drank his beer. There was something supremely sensual in the curve of his throat muscles and the bob of his Adam's apple as he swallowed. She had a sudden, crazy impulse to lean over and kiss his neck. She couldn't remember when she'd last been so attracted to a man. There was something subtly powerful about him—a kind of raw animal grace and energy she found extremely attractive.

Her left hand rested on the bar between them, palm up. Dylan startled her by reaching for her hand and pulling it closer. "I can read palms, you know," he said, staring down at her hand.

"Oh, yeah, right," Zoë replied skeptically, though she made no move to pull her hand away. There was both strength and tenderness in his touch. It was at once comforting and thrilling in a way she didn't entirely understand.

"No, really," he insisted, bending over to peer at her palm. He drew a finger along her skin. "You have a very interesting palm, did you know that?"

"Sure, I hear that all the time." Zoë tried for a playful tone, but her voice caught in her throat. She swallowed hard and managed to flash a grin.

Dylan smiled back. "Seriously. Your heart line and head line are fused. That indicates you live life with great intensity on all levels. Is that true, Zoë?" Something in his gaze, and the way he was moving his thumb in a sensual circle over the fleshy part of Zoë's palm, sent a shiver of desire rushing to her core.

She forced herself to meet Dylan's hot gaze as she struggled to form a saucy retort. No words came.

"That's all right," Dylan said, his lips lifting into a sensual smile. "You don't have to tell me now. But tell me this." He continued to trace the lines on her palm with his thumb. "How do you feel about the concept of erotic submission? Have you ever experienced the allure of leather and rope, or the sensual power of a whip's kiss? "

With a shocked gasp, Zoë pulled her hand away.

~*~

The air in the crowded bar was close, and Zoë had unbuttoned the top two buttons of her sleeveless silk blouse, giving Dylan a very nice view of the tops of her plump, rounded breasts above a hint of dark pink lace. The hem of her narrow skirt had ridden partially up her thigh as she swiveled toward him on the barstool. Her legs were long and smooth, the bare skin lightly tanned.

It was easy to imagine her naked and bound, skin glistening

with sweat, her hair wild about her face. He could almost hear her breathy cries as he cracked a whip behind her, letting its sharp tip flick over her skin, leaving behind a lovely, red welt—a symbol of her willingness to suffer for him. After she had been properly whipped, he might leave her there awhile, swaying in her bonds, her back forcibly arched by her position, her luscious nipples erect with desire. He might even let her come, not as a reward for her submission and grace during her whipping, but solely because it pleased him to take what he wanted, when he wanted.

Normally he didn't permit himself to indulge in this sort of fantasy when the subject was a vanilla girl. He'd learned from experience you couldn't force a woman into something as intense and sacred as BDSM if she wasn't properly hardwired for the experience, any more than you could force a gay person to be straight. They might go through the motions, but without the heart and mind being fully engaged, what was the point?

Zoë Stamos was one of those women it was hard to get a handle on. Admittedly, she was incredibly easy on the eyes, with her shoulder-length dark hair, luminous, liquid brown eyes and flawless skin over fine bones. She had the easy, confident physical grace of a natural athlete and a sassy, willful attitude Dylan had always found appealing in a woman. Her perfume was light but intoxicating, and he wondered how much of her scent was from a bottle, and how much was her natural feminine essence.

Until tonight he'd written her off as a typical driven young executive. One of those women who was certain she was smarter and better than any man, and determined to prove it at every possible opportunity. He suspected she approached potential sexual relationships with the same ferocity and determination to "win" with which she took on the business world.

He was enjoying their causal flirtation, but hadn't really thought much past a possible stolen kiss when they said goodnight. At least, he hadn't been. Until he'd seen her reaction to his calculated question.

It had just been a gambit without serious intent. If he hadn't had a couple of beers, he probably wouldn't have risked the exploratory tease. He'd just thrown a line into the flirtatious waters swirling between them on the off chance she might go for the bait.

She stared at him now, desire warring with shock in her expression. As if coming suddenly to herself, she looked abruptly away. With hands that trembled ever so slightly, she took a long drink of her cocktail while she attempted to compose herself. Most telling of all, her nipples had perked like gumdrops against the sheer silk of her blouse, as spontaneous as a teenage boy's sudden and uncontrollable erection when faced with a naked woman.

He'd hit a nerve—no question about it. He would play it carefully—tease her along and gauge her reaction each step of the way. It surprised him to realize how much it already mattered to him. Maybe it was the way her eyes had widened when he'd queried her directly about sensual submission. Her lips had parted with what had seemed to him unmistakable hunger, before her brain kicked into gear and censored her gut reaction. Zoë wanted what he offered—now it was just up to him to show her.

He swiveled to face her and smiled a slow, easy smile. "I take that as a no?"

Zoë set her glass carefully on the bar. She straightened her spine and lifted her chin. "I'm sure I don't know what you mean." When Dylan said nothing to this, she tossed back her glossy hair and gave a small laugh, though the smile didn't quite reach her eyes. "I mean, if you're talking the stuff of romance novels, certainly I'm aware of the concept of BDSM, but if you're talking real life..." She trailed off, and for the first time in the brief period he'd known her, seemed to be at a loss for words. Finally she continued, "Fantasy is one thing—the idea of a dominant guy swooping in and saving the poor little damsel in distress is appealing in a certain sense, I suppose. But in the real world, a woman, at least a woman who wants to get anywhere on her own, needs to stand on her own two feet, both in the bedroom and out of it." Again she tossed her hair and lifted her chin to emphasize her point. "I mean, look at me. I put together multi-million dollar ventures for a living. I deal with rich and powerful men every day of the week. The thought of letting some alpha male take over my life and control my every move is beyond absurd. I like to be in charge. It's who I am."

"Of course that's who you are. But that's not all you are."

"Meaning...?"

"Meaning being strong, self-sufficient, confident and a kickass businesswoman is not at odds with being sexually submissive and masochistic with your lover. Erotic submission is not for the weak-willed or the needy. It's not about searching for a daddy or a savior. On the contrary, it takes a strong, centered woman to make the kind of intimate, courageous connection required for a true D/s experience."

Zoë snorted. "You really believe that?"

"I don't just believe it. I live it."

Zoë stared at him, her mouth falling slightly open. She leaned toward him as if drawn by the magnetism of his words. Along with the shock, there was unmistakable hunger in her eyes.

Dylan decided to push the envelope a little further. "D/s—dominance and submission—isn't necessarily just a sexual kink. For many it's a lifestyle. And yes, part of that lifestyle includes whips and chains, along with rope, erotic suffering, sexual torture"—he watched her carefully for her reaction—"total obedience, slave training, needle play, flogging, intense bondage, forced orgasms—I could go on and on. The list is endless and endlessly delightful to explore."

Zoë's cheeks were flushed, her lips forming a small, sweet O, her eyes glittering as they moved over his face. It was a look he had seen many times before, and one that thrilled him to his core. If he leaned forward just a little, he would be close enough to kiss her.

A jarring, chirping sound came from the Zoë's suit jacket, which hung on the back of her barstool. As if released from a spell, Zoë fumbled in the jacket pocket and pulled out a cellphone. She glanced at the screen. "Sorry. I have to take this." She slid from the stool and touched the screen.

"Fuck," Dylan swore softly to himself. Talk about bad timing.

Zoë had turned away to take the call, and a sudden tension stiffened her body. She spoke in a low, urgent voice and it was evident from her tone and body language she was upset about something. Very upset. She stepped farther away from the bar, moving toward a back wall where it was less crowded. The call went on for a long time—long enough that Dylan began to forget his thwarted plans of seduction and to be a little worried for her. Was the issue business or personal? Whatever it was, the mood was ruined.

After about ten minutes, Zoë finally returned to the bar. All the light had been snuffed from her large eyes and her pretty lips were pulled down into a frown. She looked pale, even ashen, as if she'd received a very bad shock. "I have to go," she said abruptly, grabbing her jacket and bag from the back of the barstool. "Something's come up."

"What is it?" Dylan asked, concerned. "I hope everything's okay? No one's been hurt?"

She slid her eyes toward his and then away again. "No, no one's hurt. At least not physically. It's just"—she stopped herself with a resolute shake of her head. "No. Never mind. This is my problem. I'm a big girl. I'll figure this out on my own."

She started to turn away. Impulsively, Dylan reached for her arm. "Don't go. Tell me what it is, Zoë. Please. Maybe I can help. There's no reason you have to face whatever this is alone."

He was reasonably sure the issue was financial—her bearing and reaction indicated to him it was a business transaction gone awry. "Look, if this is about money, I have resources and connections. Tell me what's going on. Better yet—let's cut to the chase. How much money do you need to fix the problem?"

Zoë worked for a tiny, albeit up-and-coming, venture capital firm, so how much money could they really be talking about? A couple of million at the most? Nothing to lose sleep over, surely.

Zoë put her hands on her hips, an *I dare you* expression on her pretty face. "Six million dollars. By Tuesday afternoon."

~*~

Zoë waited for the surprise in his eyes, and then the sympathetic shrug of regret. That would be followed by a condescending remark along the lines that we can't always be winners, or if you want to play with the big boys, you have to learn to roll with the punches. Dylan Hart was well-connected through his investment banking firm, but she doubted he could lay his hands on that kind of money in two days for someone he barely knew. Or that he would want to, their highly-charged sexual banter notwithstanding.

Dylan said nothing at first. He swiveled back toward the bar and signaled for another round. Then he gestured toward the stool she had vacated. "Sit down," he finally said, "and let's discuss this." Something in his tone and his bearing made her obey.

She slid back onto the stool and reached for the fresh drink the bartender set before her. The pleasant buzz she'd had earlier had been burned away by the phone call. As she struggled to regain her composure, Zoë stole a sideline glance at Dylan.

He reminded her of the French actor, Gérard Depardieu, when the actor was very young. Like Depardieu, Dylan was broad and muscular without being especially tall. His nose was too large for his face, his jaw perhaps a bit too pronounced. He generally sported a few days' worth of stubble on his jaw, which added a rugged, sexy air to his demeanor. What made him really attractive were his eyes. They were an unusual shade of light brown—more like amber, flecked with gold.

She liked his habit, which she'd noticed during their work together, of running his hands through his thick, dark blond hair when he was concentrating on something. Distracted, he would leave it tousled and unruly, in stark contrast to the typical styled and gelled look favored by the fashionable young execs on the Street. He seemed more comfortable in jeans and work boots than a suit and tie.

If only she hadn't taken the stupid phone call. She could have gone on enjoying their sexual banter without knowing the world had just cracked open beneath her feet. No question about it—she was deep in the shit and time was most definitely not on her side. She'd put too many of her eggs in the wrong basket, and she'd done it all on her own, determined to impress her boss. She was going to impress him, all right, but not in the way she'd hoped. The humiliation of failure made her eyes burn with sudden, unshed tears and she blinked them away. Just like baseball, there was no crying on Wall Street.

Dylan was watching her, the small smile on his face kind rather than superior. She liked that he didn't prod her. Maybe he would have a suggestion or advice. Or better yet, a way out.

Zoë took a gulp of her margarita, and then another, savoring the sweet burn of the liquor as it bloomed in her chest. What the hell—there was nothing to lose, and so she admitted, "It's something I was working on on my own. I mean, I'm doing it through the firm, but Bob doesn't know about it. I was going to surprise him." She managed to muster a rueful smile. "I've wanted to broker a deal on my own for a while now, but Bob didn't think I was ready yet." She sighed, staring unhappily down into her drink. "I guess he was right."

"Hold on. Back up a minute. You've had a setback, I get that, but that kind of thing happens all the time in this business. It doesn't mean you fold up the tent and go home. It just means it's time to get creative or to call in a few favors. Tell me more about this deal. What did you put together?"

"It's a small tech firm. They're on the cusp of some amazing technology that could revolutionize mobile device battery life. They aren't quite there yet, but I've done a lot of research, and I really believe in these guys. They need funding to move forward, and I've put together a small group of investors. The deal was all set to close on Tuesday."

Dylan was regarding her with complete attention, a rare trait, and one she appreciated. Unlike most money guys, especially when talking to a woman, Dylan seemed to know how to listen, not just hold forth.

The lump that had formed in her throat during the phone call made it hard to continue, but Zoë forced herself to go on. "That was my key investor on the phone. Actually, it was his assistant. Apparently he was just indicted by a grand jury for embezzlement, and all his assets have been frozen." She shrugged miserably. "The assistant said they could *probably* get the stay lifted in a few weeks, but this deal isn't going to wait. If I can't come to the table, there are plenty of folks lined up right behind me."

"Six million?" Dylan pursed his lips, his eyes narrowing in thought. He lifted the side of his mouth in a half smile, and there was a sudden fire in his golden-brown eyes as he swept his gaze over Zoë in a way that made her somehow feel naked. She wrapped her arms around her torso and waited.

"I could get that for you by Tuesday, without question," he said slowly. The edgy, powerful intensity she'd experienced before when he'd been saying all that crazy stuff about bondage and submission was back in his tone, and in spite of the dire situation, she could feel a steady throb of desire at her core. She wanted this man. More than she'd wanted anyone in a long, long time.

His eyes boring into hers, Dylan continued, "As I say, I can get the money, but you do understand it will cost you. I plan to exact a very high price."

A jumble of confused emotions assailed Zoë at this pronouncement, and the sensual spell of a moment before evaporated in an instant. He was just another banker looking for the next quick buck. Shit. How had she misread him so completely?

She swallowed her disappointment and told herself this was for the best. She lifted her chin and asked in a businesslike tone, "What are the terms?"

Dylan didn't answer immediately. He tilted his head, regarding her in a way that made her feel hot and cold all at once. They were physically close because of the way the barstools were positioned, and she could smell his warm, masculine scent. Unable to resist his magnetic allure, she found herself leaning closer. His eyes were still locked on hers, the fire blazing behind them.

When he finally spoke, his voice was low and clear, the power beneath it impossible to ignore or resist. "I'm not talking about money. I'm talking about something altogether different."

He reached out and ran his finger along her bare arm. His touch sent an electric shiver over her skin, and she was horrified at herself when a small but audible moan came from her lips. She pressed them together and waited, her heart beating suddenly over-fast.

"I trust your financial acumen, Zoë. I'm willing to invest six million of my own money into this venture of yours. In exchange, you will spend the next forty-eight hours as my sexual slave. You will be confined to my basement dungeon, and you will be subject to my every sensual whim and erotic torture."

His hand moved over her arm to her shoulder, his fingers lightly grazing her throat. *I live it,* he had said. Zoë became aware her mouth had fallen open, but she couldn't even muster the muscle control to close it. She just stared at him as he continued, "I can see it in your eyes and your body language. You want what I'm offering."

His hand moved again, this time his fingers curling lightly around her throat. An involuntary shudder racked her body, and another moan escaped her lips. Christ, who *was* this man? "And I, in turn," Dylan continued, "want you, but only on my terms." He removed his hand and sat back on his stool, his eyes still locked on hers. Her hand fluttered to her bare throat, which felt oddly bereft of his touch. "I will never harm you when you are in my charge. I firmly believe in the concept of *safe*, *sane* and *consensual* as it applies to the BDSM lifestyle, no matter how intense our involvement might become."

Dylan turned back to the bar to pick up his beer bottle. Zoë slumped a little, as if she were a marionette and he'd just released her strings. He took a long drink while she struggled desperately to compose herself. She was at once flustered and on fire—something hot and wild had ignited inside her with his words. She had no idea how to put it out, or if she even wanted to. Was he seriously asking her for a weekend of kinky sex in exchange for an investment of such magnitude?

He leaned closer, so close his lips nearly brushed hers as he whispered, "I can promise you this, Zoë, this will be an experience you will never forget. And one you won't regret, no matter what else happens, or doesn't happen, between us."

Zoë's heart was hammering in her chest, and she found it hard to catch her breath. Her eyes fluttered shut in anticipation of his kiss.

But no kiss came.

She opened her eyes to find him regarding her with an amused, sardonic smile. "So," he said. "Do we have a deal?"

Chapter 2

Zoë's mouth worked for a moment, but no words came. He could see the struggle, the resistance and the desire at war within her. Though she couldn't possibly know the full extent of what she was going to agree to, he was nearly certain she would say yes. And not because of the promise of the cash infusion she would need to save her deal, or at least not solely because of that. He could sense the yearning, the *need* to find out what it was he was offering, and those feelings outweighed her natural trepidation.

After what seemed a long time, but he knew was in reality only a few seconds, Zoë nodded. "Yes. Okay. All right, I'll do it." She lifted her chin. "But I need proof first. I need to see that you have access to those kinds of funds, and I need to know the money will be there on Tuesday."

Dylan nodded, slipping his hand into his pocket to keep from shooting a triumphant fist into the air. He swallowed for the same reason—to buy himself a little time so he didn't burst out with something stupid like, "All-fucking-right!" Instead, keeping his voice calm, he said soberly, "Fair enough. Let's go over to my office, and I'll get things set up."

He paid the bar tab, and they stepped out together into the warm summer evening. As they walked the three city blocks to his office building, Zoë told him more about the details and structure of her deal. As she talked, she became increasingly animated and excited, and Dylan understood just how important it was for her not only to close the deal, but to prove to the world and, probably most importantly, to herself, that she had what it took to make it in high finance.

"I want this more than anything I've ever wanted in my life," she said earnestly. "I've been working on this every spare minute for the last six months, and I think I have the downside covered, even if things don't pan out quite as we hope. You'll end up making money on this deal, I can almost guarantee it."

"I have to admit, Zoë, I'm quite impressed with your financial creativity and clear-minded analysis of the risks and rewards. Yes, it's a gamble, but what business deal worth doing doesn't involve some risk? You know what they say"—he shrugged and grinned, thinking of the millions he'd made, and sometimes lost, over his career—"nothing ventured, nothing gained."

They arrived at his office building, checked in with the night attendant and glided upward in the large, wood-paneled elevator, neither saying a word as they watched the digital numbers rise. Once in the empty office, he booted up his computer, and Zoë accessed the account information he would need to transfer the promised money. It took about a half hour to complete the various transactions necessary to liquidate the needed funds. Once he was done, Dylan called to Zoë, who had been staring out of the huge glass windows that framed Manhattan's famous night-lit skyline, to come over to his desk.

"There it is," he said, pointing to the scheduled transfer. "All set and ready to go. Once you complete your end of the deal"—he paused, letting his eyes sweep slowly over her face and body, amused and aroused at the faint flush of pink rising to her cheeks—"the money will be sent to your account."

Zoë wrapped her arms protectively around herself and bit her lower lip.

Dylan lifted his brows as he regarded her. "What? Having second thoughts? It's not too late—you want out"—he offered an exaggerated shrug—"I'm sure you can find the funding elsewhere. The deal is solid. I would hate to think I was forcing you into something you didn't really want to do."

Zoë said nothing, instead continuing to worry her lower lip. Dylan resisted the urge to pull her into his arms and bite that sexy, pouty lip himself. Instead, he added softly, "Forty-eight hours, Zoë. Two uninterrupted days to discover if your secret desires can become reality." He reached for her shoulders then, and stared deeply into her eyes. "I want it," he admitted, letting the urgency he felt slip into his tone. "I think you want it too."

She stared back and finally nodded. "Yes," she whispered. "Yes, I want it too."

They took the elevator down to the parking garage, where Dylan's silver BMW M5 waited like a gallant steed to carry them home. They stopped first at Zoë's midtown apartment. He waited out front while she went up to collect her toiletries and do whatever else she needed for her weekend stay. "You won't need any clothing," he said, again enjoying the sweet blush his words provoked, "so pack lightly."

Once they wove their way out of the crush of city traffic, Dylan made good time. He glanced over at Zoë as he drove along Bronx River Parkway toward his Scarsdale home. She was quiet, her eyes on the road, her hands twisting nervously in her lap. It was after eleven, but he wasn't the least bit tired, or if he was, the adrenaline kicking around like rocket fuel in his gut wouldn't let him realize it.

What an extraordinary opportunity. The whole concept of taking an innocent—a total neophyte in the world of BDSM—and introducing her to its dark pleasures and infinite intensity, had completely taken him over since it had leaped full-blown into his brain at the bar. Zoë was a blank slate with the potential, he sensed, to become a masterpiece of erotic submission and grace. She had no preconceived notions, no negative experience to undo.

He slowed as he exited the highway and wended his way through the large, tree-lined streets of his quiet neighborhood. He pulled into his driveway and pressed the garage door remote on the visor. He eased the car into its space, turned off the engine, and turned to face his lovely, willing captive. She was still staring straight ahead, her hands now clenched into fists on either thigh.

"You all right?" Dylan touched Zoë's shoulder, and she flinched.

"Hey, it's all good, you know?" he said gently. She said nothing. "Zoë, look at me." Slowly she turned her head in his direction, her dark eyes wide, her lower lip caught between her teeth. Dylan stroked her cheek. "Listen to me, Zoë. It's not too late to turn around and forget this whole thing." Dylan could barely admit to himself how much her response mattered. He waited a beat, but she still said nothing.

He took her hand, and she didn't pull away. She stared down at their hands, as if tracing the lines in her mind. "I'm going to ask you something, Zoë, and I want you to answer honestly."

Zoë looked up again. "What?" she whispered.

"Something happened between us back at the bar. I know you have no experience with BDSM and the power of erotic submission, but I sensed something in you—a direct and immediate response, even yearning, for the potential of what I'm offering you this weekend. The Dom in me connected on a gut level to the sub in you. Even if this business deal didn't exist, I find I want—no, let me go even further—I *need* to explore your submissive potential with you. This is an amazing opportunity for us both—a full forty-eight hours with no outside distractions, no other commitments, and none of the usual emotional complications of a new relationship to navigate in the process. It will just be you and me—no pretense, no artifice, no games. Even without the promise of investment money, I sense that, on some level, you want this as much as I do. Am I wrong?"

The world stood still as he waited for her answer.

"No," she said at last in a low but clear voice. "You're not wrong. Something happened back in the bar when you were saying those things to me. At first I thought you were just trying to shock me, but even if that were the case, the words somehow bypassed my brain and went right to my"—she broke off, her cheeks reddening. She laughed nervously and tossed back her hair—"my body. Or not even just my body, but my..."

"Your soul," Dylan provided, forcing himself to stay calm and centered, sensing this was the moment they would seal the deal, or it would fall to pieces.

"Yes," she whispered, and then louder, "Yes."

Just to be absolutely sure, Dylan reiterated, "Then you're prepared to honor the terms of our agreement? You will submit to me fully for the duration of this weekend? You agree to be my sexual submissive, to accept, endure and embrace my training, and to trust I will keep you safe from harm, but know I will push every erotic and sensual boundary you possess?"

Zoë drew in a deep breath and let it out slowly. She nodded. "I do."

"You need to understand that once you step out of this car, your will is no longer your own. For the duration of the weekend, I will decide when you sleep, when you eat, when you use the bathroom, when you receive pleasure and when you endure pain. You will be directed, controlled, sexually used, bound, erotically tortured, and exhaustively trained in the art of submission."

Zoë had stopped twisting her hands. They rested easily on her lap, and while he could feel her excitement and the tension of expectation, he could sense her determination. All the marks of a true sub were plain on her face and in her bearing. She was born to this, even if she didn't know it yet.

Her words bore out his belief. "Yes. I agree to the terms."

Dylan barely acknowledged to himself the relief that flooded through his being at her pronouncement. "Good," he said. "Then it begins. Now."

Zoë started to reach for the door handle, but Dylan said, "Wait. Before we go in, I want to go over a few rules and regulations." She let her hand fall away and turned once more to regard him. "First of all," he continued, "slave girls don't wear clothing in my house. That means you will strip here in the garage. You can leave your clothes in the car, and I'll collect them for you later."

Zoë opened her mouth as if to protest. Dylan shook his head. "Shh, no talking. That's the second rule. Slave girls do not speak unless asked a direct question. When you do speak, you will address me as Sir. For the duration of the weekend, I am not Dylan. I am Sir to you. Is that understood?"

Again there was a long pause. Zoë's cheeks were still flushed and her eyes were fever-bright. "Yes, Sir," she finally said, her low sultry voice and the import of her words sending a jolt of hot desire directly to his cock.

~*~

I can't believe I'm doing this, I can't believe I'm doing this.

Even as these words looped endlessly through her mind, Zoë slipped off her shoes. It being summer, she wore no stockings, and the cement floor was cool beneath her bare feet. Dylan stood nearby, watching her as she undressed, his expression implacable, save for the spark of lust and power in his golden-brown eyes.

When she was down to her bra and panties, she hesitated, her gut clenching with nerves. It wasn't that she was shy about her body, but it felt so inequitable to be stripping naked for this virtual stranger while he stood there, her overnight bag in his hand, watching her every move.

Dylan cocked an eyebrow, waiting. Blowing out a breath, Zoë reached back and unhooked her bra, letting it fall forward on her arms. He didn't look away as she pulled down her panties and stepped carefully out of them. She laid her things on the car seat and closed the door, standing uncertainly in front of the man who would dictate her every move for the next two days.

It was as if he had stepped out of an erotic romance novel, brought to life by her secret, barely acknowledged longing for something more. But those were just dark, sexy words on a page designed to fuel her fantasies when she masturbated late at night, alone in her bed and in search of release. This was no fantasy, and Dylan was no paper hero. He was flesh and blood—a real man with his own agenda.

I can't believe I'm doing this, I can't believe I'm doing this.

And yet, if she were totally honest with herself, she wanted to do it. And not just to secure the investment funds. He was right, though she had no idea how he knew—his words and promises had resonated, connecting to something bright and fierce at the core of her being.

Dylan punched numbers into a keypad on the door. He turned the knob and flicked on the light. They stepped into a large kitchen equipped with the expected stainless steel appliances, granite countertops and ceramic-tiled flooring. Dylan led her to a bar and directed that she sit. She perched on the edge of the barstool and wrapped her arms around herself.

"Are you cold?" Dylan asked, regarding her. "I can raise the thermostat."

She shook her head. "No, I'm good...Sir," she added after a moment.

He smiled and moved to the refrigerator. He took out a

bottle of white wine and placed it on the counter. Opening a cabinet door, he removed two crystal wine glasses, which he set beside the bottle.

Extracting the cork, he poured wine into each glass and turned toward her, both glasses in his hands. He held one out to her, and Zoë took it gratefully, in need of a bit of liquid courage. She drank the fruity, crisp wine in two gulps. Dylan lifted an eyebrow and held out the bottle. He'd barely sipped from his own glass. "A little more?"

"Yes, please…Sir," Zoë said, offering her empty glass. He filled it again, and this time she sipped more slowly. Dylan took some things out of the refrigerator as she sipped, and in a moment he placed a plate of sliced cheese and crackers before her. Zoë realized she was hungry, the pizza they'd all shared at the bar hours before now a distant memory.

She ate a few of the crackers topped with cheese and had more of the wine. It was surreal in the extreme to be sitting there naked as a jaybird in this man's kitchen. The quiet but persistent mantra of incredulity at what she had committed herself to spooled in a continuous loop through her brain: *I can't believe I'm doing this, I can't believe I'm doing this.*

Finally Dylan said, "It's time, Zoë. Your submission begins now. Stand up with your arms at your sides."

Zoë's heart instantly kicked into high gear and her legs wobbled a little as she stood from the barstool. *In for a penny, in for a pound*, she reminded herself.

Reaching into a drawer, Dylan pulled out what looked like a dog collar and a leash. The collar was red and made of thick, sturdy canvas, held closed with a Velcro strap. He pulled the Velcro open and brought the collar to her throat. Instinctively, Zoë took a step back.

"I didn't tell you to move," Dylan said quietly. "Stay as you are. You will wear this collar for the duration of your stay here. It is both a symbol of your servitude, and a useful device for securing you."

Humiliation surged through Zoë, warming her face as Dylan wrapped the collar around her throat. A part of her wanted to smack his hands away and retort that she was not a *dog*, for god's sake, and would not wear anybody's collar. But an odd thing happened as he pressed the Velcro closed. A melting heat spread through her body and stiffened her nipples. Without meaning to, she touched the collar, tugging gently against its confines, a small voice whispering from some secret place, *yes*.

Dylan clipped the metal leash to the O-ring at the center of the collar and gave it an experimental tug, pulling Zoë forward a step. Again her mind wanted to rebel, to retort, to demand, but instead she only moaned softly, her clit pulsing with need.

He reached for her overnight bag, which he'd set on the floor by the counter. As he slung it over his shoulder, he said, "It's late and it's been a long day. Come, I'll show you where you'll be staying."

He led her by the leash out of the kitchen into a narrow room just beside it that she recognized from her grandparents' old house as a butler's pantry. At the back of the pantry was a door, which opened to reveal a descending staircase. She gripped the bannister as he led her slowly down the smooth wooden steps.

The basement floor was cement and the room was empty, save for a fancy washer and dryer set and a counter with a sink. He led her past the washer and dryer to a door at the back of the room.

He turned the deadbolt beneath the knob and pushed open the door. The thick red carpet inside the room was soft beneath her bare feet. "For the next forty-eight hours," Dylan said in his deep, sexy voice, "this space will become your world. You will eat here, sleep here, bathe here"—he pointed toward another smaller room visible through an open doorframe from which the door itself had been removed—"and train here. You exist only to serve me from this point on. You are my property to train and to use as I see fit."

There was a twin bed in the corner of the room covered in a white sheet, a white duvet folded at the foot, a single pillow at its head. All sorts of strange equipment filled the rest of the space, including a large wooden X cross with cuffs chained to each of its four corners. There was a padded bench covered in black leather, more cuffs secured along its perimeter. A large animal cage stood along the wall opposite the bed with newspaper and a water bowl inside it, making Zoë wonder if Dylan kept a pet. He must have been following her gaze, because he said, "That's the punishment cage."

"My god," Zoë whispered faintly, a shudder of trepidation moving through her frame. For the first time, the full import of what she'd agreed to hit her like a sledgehammer. She hadn't told a soul where she was. Clearly this wasn't the first time Dylan had used this room. What if women went down here willingly enough, but never came out? What if she'd just walked into the lair of a madman? What if tonight was her last on earth?

"Hey," Dylan said softly. "Calm down. Breathe." He unclipped the leash from her collar and put his arm around her. Despite the possibility he was a serial killer, Zoë leaned into his comforting embrace. He guided her to the bed and she sat, suddenly nearly overwhelmed with exhaustion.

Dylan pressed her gently back against the pillow. He cupped her cheek, his voice still gentle, his eyes kind. "I understand you're completely new to this. I expect obedience and grace, but I don't expect perfection. Because of our limited time, the experience will be intense and fast-paced. I will correct you when you err, but by the same token, I will reward you when you succeed."

His hand moved from her cheek to her neck, his fingers curling lightly around her throat just above the loose collar. Again a tremor moved through her body at his touch and she began to tremble, though not from fear, but rather from a strange, quaking desire she herself didn't understand.

His hand still on her throat, he lowered his head and his lips found hers. The kiss was gentle at first—an exploration, a whisper of promised passion. Then his tongue pressed itself between her lips. He tasted of the wine they'd shared, and his tongue was warm and wet against hers. His hand tightened at her throat as he kissed her, his other hand cupping her breast. His fingers moved over her skin, finding her nipple. His mouth still locked on hers, his one hand still tight on her throat, he pinched her nipple with his other hand, and then twisted it, sending a sudden, sharp explosion of pain through her nerve endings.

She gasped against his mouth, instinctively struggling to pull away, but his hands and mouth held her firmly in place. Her nipple continued to throb as his fingers drifted down her torso, moving over her belly to her sex, which was hot and swollen between her legs. She moaned against his mouth as he slipped a large, hard finger into her wet cunt, his palm pressing against her aching clit.

His kiss, his masterful touch, the wine, the whole crazy situation—it all combined to pull her completely out of herself. He stroked, teased and kissed her until she lost all sense of time, space and even consciousness. She became pure sensation, and she gave herself wholly to the experience.

Her body began to buck and spasm, her hips rising from the mattress as she ground wantonly against Dylan's powerful hand. She heard her own piercing keen of pleasure, but she was too far gone to do anything whatsoever about it. When his touch was finally withdrawn, she fell back against the bed, utterly spent, gasping for breath, her heart pounding, her entire body thrumming from perhaps the most powerful orgasm she'd ever experienced.

After a while, she had no idea how long, she finally managed to open her eyes. Dylan was regarding her with a bemused smile, his eyes glowing with a powerful inner fire that at once thrilled and frightened her. "That one was free," he said. "Going forward, you'll need to remember rule number three, which is that for duration of our time together, I own your body and your orgasms. You will never touch yourself without permission, and you will not come until I tell you to."

He pointed to a small gray plastic case with a glass eye that was installed high in a corner of the room. "That's a closed-circuit camera that encompasses the entire room. It's both for safety and for surveillance, so I'll know if you misbehave, little girl." He pressed his open palm gently against her bare mons, his touch sending a shuddering aftershock through her frame.

Leaning over her, he kissed the tip of her nose. "Now, get some rest." He pushed himself to his feet and stood, staring down at her. "You may use the bathroom and wash up." He nodded toward her overnight bag, which he'd dropped just inside the door. "I'll be down bright and early, so I would recommend you go straight to sleep."

He walked to the door and stopped, turning back toward her. "Welcome to paradise, slave girl. Just watch out for snakes." With that, he exited the room and closed the door.

She heard the sound of the deadbolt being slipped into place, and then the room was plunged into darkness. She lay there awhile in a kind of dazed stupor. As her eyes adjusted, she realized there was in fact light coming from the bathroom, which reminded her she needed to pee.

Rolling from the bed, she stood and moved toward the light. The bathroom was small, with barely room for a toilet, sink and shower stall. There was a large nightlight plugged into an outlet over the sink, and it was enough to see by. She lowered herself to the toilet.

She had forgotten to get her overnight bag, but was too exhausted to got get it. She would brush her teeth and shower in the morning. Now all she wanted to do was pass out into oblivion. There was too much—way too much—to process tonight. Her brain had short-circuited from the overload of sensation, and it was all she could do to remain conscious. She splashed water on her face and left the bathroom.

She sank down onto the bed and reached for the coverlet. Before she even had it all the way up, she was asleep.

Chapter 3

Zoë opened her eyes and stared for several seconds at the cement ceiling overhead. As her brain clicked on, she sat bolt upright, seeking the new source of light in the windowless room. It was coming from the bathroom, but it wasn't the yellow glow of the nightlight. Curious, she slid her legs over the side of the bed and made her way to the bathroom.

There was a small window placed high along the wall that she hadn't noticed the night before. Closing the lid of the toilet, she climbed onto it to get a better view. She could see a finely-kept lawn at eye-level, and the base of several fat, old tree trunks in the distance. Between them she could glimpse patches of pink and gold sky. The clock in her head informed her it was somewhere close to five in the morning, but she didn't feel in the least tired. There was too much adrenaline zinging through her system to even contemplate the thought of going back to sleep.

She used the toilet and then retrieved her overnight bag. As she brushed her teeth, she pondered the surreal nature of her situation. She had willingly consigned herself to be this man's sex slave for the next two days. A small part of her mind was attempting to admonish her over her foolish willingness to put herself into another's hands so completely, but the greater part of her was excited at the chance to surrender to something she had never thought would be more than an idle sexual fantasy tucked away at the back of her brain.

In addition to the undeniable sexual attraction she felt both toward the man and what he offered, Zoë thrilled to a challenge. She was determined to face and conquer this as she had every challenge in her life.

Glancing into the mirror over the sink, she whispered fiercely, "Bring it on, Hart," even as her stomach did an uncomfortable loop-de-loop of nervous anticipation.

She rummaged in her bag and silently cursed herself when she realized she'd forgotten her shampoo and conditioner. As she turned on the water, she was both gratified and disconcerted to see that the shower already contained these items, along with a fresh bar of soap and a disposable razor. How many women before her had stayed in this basement dungeon, and for how long?

She stood beneath the shower's spray, her face lifted to its warmth as the water splashed over her. The electric lights suddenly blazed on, startling her enough to make her gasp in surprise. She heard the scrape of the deadbolt turning.

"Zoë? Where are you?"

She heard his footsteps and a moment later Dylan appeared in the doorway of the bathroom. She grabbed for the towel, confused and disoriented by his sudden appearance.

"Give me that towel. Step out of the shower and lift your arms over your head."

"Excuse me? I'm not done. I barely started."

"I said get out." His tone and the look on his face left no room for argument. Alarmed, Zoë held out the towel and stepped hastily from of the shower.

"Arms over your head," he repeated as he took the towel from her.

Blushing, flustered and annoyed to have been interrupted, Zoë nevertheless did as she was told. Dylan used the towel, his touch surprisingly gentle as he buffed and dried her body and hair. "I must not have been clear last night, or perhaps you just weren't paying attention. For the duration of the weekend, I decide when you eat, sleep, use the toilet, and yes, when you shower as well. You will have the opportunity to groom later. First I have a few other things in mind for you."

Zoë followed Dylan out of the small bathroom, wrapping her arms nervously around her body as she walked.

Dylan stopped in the center of the room and regarded her. "Drop your arms," he ordered. "You must never hide your body from me."

Zoë dropped her arms and regarded the man she'd willingly accepted as her "Master" for the weekend. His dark blond hair curled damply around his ears—so he'd permitted *himself* to shower, while denying her. He was dressed in blue running shorts, his torso and feet bare. The sculpted muscles of his chest and abdomen reinforced her initial thought of him as a bull in a ring. The guy was ripped, pure and simple. Zoë realized she was staring, and abruptly shifted her gaze to his face.

If he'd noticed her ogling his body, thankfully he gave no indication. "Put your hands behind your head and lace your fingers at your neck, like this." Dylan demonstrated, and Zoë copied his movements, her nipples tingling to erection as he watched her.

"Good. Now, feet shoulder-width apart." He paused a beat while she obeyed, and then continued, "I call that the at-attention position. When I tell you to stand at attention, this is what I expect. You will remain in that position until given permission to move. Got it?"

Zoë nodded. The position made her feel even more naked than she had a moment before, if such a thing were possible.

"What?" Dylan snapped. "I didn't hear you."

"Yes, Sir," Zoë quickly replied, startled by the sudden brusqueness in his tone.

"Better," he said, his tone again gentle.

He walked toward a rack of scary-looking whips set against the wall. Hanks of neatly coiled rope and lengths of thick, sturdy chain hung on the wall above. Dylan selected a long-handled riding crop from the rack. Turning to face her, he added, "From this moment forward, I will correct you for that kind of slip-up. I find a quick smack of the riding crop to be more effective than words." He smacked the leather flap at the end of the crop suddenly against his own thigh.

The thwacking sound startled Zoë into saying, "Oh!" She pressed her lips quickly together, hoping the sound wouldn't be regarded as a "slip-up" in need of "correction." Dylan arched an eyebrow and tapped his thigh once more with the crop, but that was all.

Zoë gave herself a stern reminder to keep quiet unless spoken to, and to remain in position at all costs, not just because he'd told her she must, but as a matter of pride. She would totally ace this BDSM challenge and save her venture capital deal in the process.

"I gathered from our conversation last night that you know next to nothing about BDSM," Dylan said, "so I'm going to start at the beginning. Granted, we'll move far more quickly than we might if we had more time."

He pointed toward the large X-shaped cross. "Do you know what that is?"

Zoë followed the trajectory of his finger with her gaze. From her reading, she was pretty sure she was seeing an actual St. Andrew's cross but she wasn't about to admit the level of her knowledge, academic or otherwise. "It's a cross of some kind...Sir." How strange it felt to call this man who was of her own generation, a colleague she'd worked with as an equal, "Sir". And yet, as odd as it was to admit, each time she said the word, it sent a jolt of excitement directly to her cunt. She eyed the cuffs dangling from the corners of the cross, adding, "It's a restraining device."

Dylan nodded. "Correct. It's called a St. Andrew's cross. You'll see one in most BDSM dungeons. It's ideal for quick, thorough restraint. It's handy when you don't have the ability to suspend your slave from the ceiling."

He pointed upward, and Zoë experienced a small shock and another jolt to her cunt as she took in the large eyebolts screwed into the thick support beam. Her imagination instantly placed her beneath it, her arms stretched taut overhead by ropes secured to the eyebolts, her body spread and exposed for whatever diabolical torture this man might devise for her. A shudder moved through her frame at the image, and Dylan's lips curled into a cruel, sensual smile, his gold-flecked eyes glittering as if he, too, were imagining her there.

Still holding the riding crop, Dylan strode to the whip rack and selected an ominous-looking black whip with a long, wicked tail. He flicked it suddenly, and the resulting sonic crack startled Zoë to such an extent that she dropped her arms from their position behind her head, her right hand instinctively flying up to cover her mouth.

Dylan regarded her with a shake of his head. "Bad girl." He strode to her in a few quick strides. Before she could react, the riding crop smacked against her bare ass three times in quick, stinging succession.

She yelped in outraged surprise and jumped away. "Hey! What're you doing?" she demanded, the words leaping out of her mouth before she could stop them. "Oh!" she blurted. "I'm sorry, Sir!" Hastily she resumed the at-attention position, her face hot with humiliation, her bottom tingling painfully from the crop.

Dylan regarded her for several silent moments while she struggled to regain her composure. "Why did I correct you, Zoë?" he finally said.

The heat in Zoë's face intensified, but she knew she had to reply. "Because I fell out of position, Sir," she forced herself to say, surprised how difficult it was to admit failure. "And I spoke out of turn."

"Will it happen again?"

"No, Sir."

"Good girl." He moved closer, so close she could smell the soap on his freshly-washed skin. "Tell me, Zoë," he said softly. "Have you ever been restrained? Cuffed with your arms overhead, completely vulnerable and defenseless?"

Another shudder moved through Zoë's frame, and she swallowed hard as she struggled to collect herself. "No, Sir." Her eyes slid involuntarily toward the back wall where the rope and chain hung, waiting.

Dylan followed her gaze, and a slow, sensual smile lifted his lips. The smile recalled to her the kiss of the night before—his mouth claiming hers as his fingers roamed her body. Her heart was beating fast, and the pulse of it throbbed at her clit.

As if privy to her secret desires, Dylan slowly shook his head. "Not yet, Zoë. You aren't yet ready for that level of restraint."

The surge of relief at this pronouncement was nearly overcome by a strange disappointment. Stunned at her own reaction, but nearly powerless against it, Zoë had to press her lips together once more to keep from blurting, "*Yes, I am so ready*," like some petulant child being denied a privilege. She stood silently, confusion roiling through her.

Dylan reached into his pocket and pulled out a silky black sash. He held it in one hand, running his fingers along the length of it with his other. The gesture was sensual in the extreme. "Have you ever been blindfolded, Zoë?"

"No, Sir," she managed to reply, her eyes fixed on his thick, blunt fingers stroking the sash.

"As our first exercise," Dylan said as he moved to stand

behind her, "we're going to play a game you may remember from your childhood. It's called Trust." He tapped her interlaced hands lightly, adding, "Drop your arms to your sides for this exercise."

Zoë obeyed, relieved to lower her arms, which had been starting to ache.

"In the game called Trust, one person stands behind the other"—as he spoke, he brought the sash around her head, securing it over her eyes and tying it behind her—"with his arms out. The one in front falls backward, trusting the other to catch her before she crashes to the floor. Are you familiar with the game, Zoë?"

The blindfold achieved its purpose of plunging her into sudden darkness. She was off-balance, and her heart was thumping so loudly she was sure Dylan must hear it. "Yes, Sir," she managed, her voice trembling slightly. "We played it at camp." She didn't add that she was never any good at it. Oh, she was fine being the catcher, but she had never mastered the ability to just let go and trust that someone, even Corrine, her very best friend in the world all through school, would actually be there to break her fall.

She jumped a little as Dylan's hands gripped her shoulders. "Relax," he whispered. "Tension is a form of resistance." Zoë let out a sigh of pleasure as his skilled fingers loosened muscles she hadn't been aware she was tensing.

After a while, his hands slid forward and down to cup her breasts. Her nipples jutted against his palms. He must feel her pounding heart. She drew in a deep breath and forced herself to let it out slowly.

"The game," he said softly, his mouth close to her ear, "contains an element of danger. You risk that the other person won't catch you and you'll fall. It can be a difficult game, but when the falling player trusts the catcher enough to let go completely, the experience for both is a moment of exhilaration that's difficult to duplicate."

He let her breasts go, his hands gliding upward along her breastbone. She gasped as one hand curled lightly around her throat above the loose dog collar, as he had done the night before when he kissed her.

"BDSM provides the same kind of exhilaration." Dylan's grip on her throat made her knees feel weak, as if she might crumple to the ground if he let her go. He placed his other hand on the small of her back, the touch warm and steadying, the combined effect at once confusing and thrilling. "When trust trumps the possibility of harm, the result is incredibly intimate and erotic. Those who have the courage and honesty to engage in a true power exchange share the most nurturing and intimate bond possible."

He kissed her neck and Zoë shivered, unable to stop herself from leaning into his touch. She had to bite back a cry of dismay when he stepped back, his hands falling away.

"Can you do it, Zoë? Can you let go and fall back into my arms? I will not let you fall. I promise."

Zoë tried to picture herself falling back into Dylan's arms. The tension he'd eased out of her shoulders a moment before recoiled in her muscles, even as she gave herself a direct order to follow through. *You can do this. You can totally do this. Just let go. He'll catch you. You know he will.*

She leaned back, waiting for gravity to aid her in her effort. She found herself grateful for the blindfold—it blotted everything out but the moment, giving her a focus she might not otherwise have. She could feel Dylan waiting patiently behind her. She imagined his strong arms spread, his large hands open on either side of her, waiting to wrap her into a safe, warm embrace as she fell back against him.

Nothing happened. Her body had turned into stone. She couldn't move a muscle.

"Zoë?"

Tears of frustration pricked her eyelids behind the blindfold. "I can't," she muttered. "I can't do it."

She waited for the anger, the reproach, the "correction." But all he said was, "Don't worry, Zoë. Trust is a two-way street. If it's meant to be, we'll get there together."

~*~

Dylan would have been stunned if Zoë had in fact managed to complete the trust exercise so quickly out of the gate. He had already observed the hard, protective shell she'd probably spent a lifetime unconsciously building around her emotions, and he'd have been amazed if she'd managed to lower it on her own with a man she barely knew.

Since he'd joined The Vault, a members-only BDSM club for serious players committed to the lifestyle, Dylan had trained a number of submissives. As a part of the training, he'd often used that particular exercise to get a sense of a new sub's level of trust and ease. He'd found even eager, willing sub girls who expressed a strong desire to submit sometimes had trouble with the Trust game.

Zoë was an unknown quantity at this point, despite his near-certainty of a submissive nature hidden beneath the accomplished and driven businesswoman persona she presented to the world. In a way, her innocence regarding the scene was a plus. She didn't come to him with preconceived notions of how a Dom should behave, and what she could expect. It was all shiny and new.

He sensed her tension and her fear, but also her excitement. His initial assessment of her submissive potential hadn't lessened. If anything, he was surer than ever. The next exercise he had planned would help him gauge the masochistic aspect of her psyche, and just the thought of it made his cock hard.

He regarded her standing before him, the blindfold covering her eyes, her hands hanging loosely at her sides. She fidgeted a little—shifting from foot to foot, her tongue flicking nervously over her lips, but otherwise doing quite well at just doing nothing, especially given her complete lack of training.

He moved slowly around her, admiring her long, lean curves and the high heft of her well-rounded breasts. Her nipples were fully erect and flushed a deep red against the creamy white of her skin where no sun had kissed it. The tailored business suits she had worn during their professional time together, while elegant and flattering, had mostly hidden her lush and curvaceous femininity.

Stepping behind her, Dylan removed the blindfold. Tucking the sash back into his pocket, he moved to face her. She blinked rapidly as her eyes readjusted to the light. Her eyes locked on his, her full lips slightly pursed, as if she were waiting for a kiss.

Distracted by that lush mouth, Dylan had to force himself to focus. "We're going to engage in some pretty intense scenes over the course of the weekend, and though I will pay close attention to your body and your reactions, sometimes a Dom can miss distress signals, and has to be hit over the head, metaphorically speaking. That's where a safeword comes in. When you use the word, it stops all action immediately and completely. Just be aware—a safeword shouldn't be used lightly. It's like the fire alarm behind the glass—for emergencies only. That said, if you're panicking during a scene and I don't seem to be picking up on your cues, you can use the word, and all action will cease."

Zoë's eyes had widened as he spoke, her breath quickening, her hands clenching and unclenching at her sides. Dylan put his hands on her shoulders and looked deep into those beautiful, dark eyes. "Hey, calm down. I've been in the scene for over a decade. I should tell you, no sub has ever had to use her safeword with me. Ever."

By the same token, no woman he'd worked with before had signed on for training in exchange for investment money, without any *real* indication they were submissive. What if he was reading her wrong, and she had only gone along with this whole thing to get the money she needed to complete her deal?

Not for the first time since he'd made the impulsive agreement, Dylan wondered if he was insane. He took the gift of erotic submission seriously, and would never dream of pushing his sexual agenda on a woman who wasn't one hundred percent willing.

But Zoë could have said no. She could have refused—he'd given her the opportunity to back out of the deal, but she'd steadfastly stuck to her guns. Despite the unorthodox nature of their arrangement, Dylan remained convinced Zoë was a sub in need of a D/s deflowering. And damn if he wasn't just the Dom to do it.

This mental pep talk took only a few seconds to register and, newly resolved, Dylan continued, "We'll choose a word together. Something from the world of high finance would be fitting. Do you have a suggestion of a word you can easily remember that has nothing to do with BDSM?"

"Buyout," Zoë offered without hesitation.

"Buyout it is," Dylan agreed.

Taking a step back, he reached for the O-ring at the center of her collar and gave it a little tug. "Come on. Let's go over to the bed. I'm going to sit with my feet on the floor, and you're going to lie over my lap, facedown. Do you know why?"

"No, Sir," she whispered, swallowing hard. Her nipples, he noted, were still fully erect.

"Because I'm going to spank you."

Her mouth opened into an O, matching the sound she made, which was long and drawn out. "Ooooooh." The response could have been prompted either by fear or desire, or maybe it was both.

She was so fucking hot, and it was all he could do not to throw her on the rug in that instant and plunge his aching cock into her heat.

Instead, his finger looped through the O-ring, he guided her to the bed. Letting her go, he sat. She stood uncertainly before him. "Have you ever been spanked? I'm not talking about parental swats. I'm talking about a lover holding you down and smacking that gorgeous ass of yours."

"No, Sir!" Zoë replied with such vehemence Dylan had to chuckle.

Dylan patted his leg. "Come on, now. Do as you're told."

Zoë held herself tentatively over him. He helped her into position, shifting her body until her sexy little bottom was perched on his thighs, her upper half resting along the mattress.

She held herself tight as a bowstring. Dylan stroked her back. "Relax. I think you'll find this a very sensuous experience, if you open yourself to it. I'll start by warming the skin, and I'll steadily increase the intensity to gauge your pain tolerance levels, okay?"

"Is it going to hurt?" Zoë's normally low, sultry voice rose nearly to a squeak, and again Dylan smiled, though this time he managed to keep the chuckle at bay. He didn't want to her to think he was making fun of her, but she was so adorable.

"Yes," he replied. "That's the idea, Zoë. It's supposed to hurt, but the experience isn't designed just to inflict pain for its sake. This is what we call 'erotic pain' and it has a very specific purpose. Actually it serves a lot of purposes at once. One is the giving of yourself over to another person—allowing them the intimacy of using your body in a way you wouldn't normally allow.

"Then there is the focus on the actual sensations—the feel

of my hand on your skin, of the blood rushing to the surface, of your muscles tensing and moving, and then ultimately relaxing as you stop resisting and learn to let go. The goal is to give yourself over to both the experience and your Dom. It can be extraordinarily liberating."

He was silent a moment as he tried to come up with an analogy she might understand. His hands moved over her soft, supple skin, his cock hard as steel beneath her naked body. "Think about a strenuous hike up a difficult mountain," he finally said. "By the end, you're drenched with sweat, every muscle aches, brambles and thorns have scraped your skin. Then you reach the summit, and a new feeling takes over. You experience this incredible exhilaration to have made it to the top, and you can hardly believe the sheer beauty and power of the vista spreading before you. And the difficult journey to that point makes the achievement all the sweeter and more meaningful. That's what a successful BDSM scene is like, not just for the receiver, but for the giver as well."

He struck her ass lightly with his open palm, the slapping sound of skin on skin echoing in the air. Zoë stiffened and jerked beneath his touch. "Ouch!" she squealed, though he knew he hadn't hurt her, only startled her.

"Relax," he urged, striking her again, just a little harder. "Let yourself begin the journey. Feel the sensations without judgment. Accept the pain." He struck her once more. "Embrace it." He kept his other hand on her lower back, both to steady her and to provide the comfort of touch.

At first she continued to squirm and tense. She was breathing rapidly, her breath ragged and shallow. "Breathe," he urged. "Stop resisting, Zoë. It's much easier to take when you open yourself to receive. Take this first step with me." He began to smack her in a steady rain of rapid strokes, alternating cheeks until the skin began to darken to a pretty pink.

After a while, he was very pleased to note her squirming had stopped, though her hands were clenched into tight fists at her sides. "Relax your hands," he said. "Uncurl your fingers and try to slow your breathing."

He wasn't sure she had heard him, but after several long beats, her fingers unfurled. She drew in a long, shuddering breath and let it out.

Encouraged, Dylan drew back his arm, cupped his palm, and gave her the first real smack, smashing down so her groin ground against his. Over and over he struck her with force, giving her the kind of spanking that would send a trained sub flying within minutes.

She tensed again beneath the onslaught, squirming and whimpering, and crying out, "Ouch! It hurts! Stop, oh stop!"

He didn't stop.

She didn't say her safeword.

He spoke in a low, calming voice near her ear. "You're doing great, Zoë. You can do this. You're almost there." He continued the spanking, watching her skin darken from pink to red, careful to keep up the intensity without taking it too far, too fast.

And then it happened.

All at once the resistance went out of her. Someone not

familiar with the masochistic sensibility might have thought she'd merely given up, but Dylan knew otherwise. Her breathing had slowed, her hands rested easily by her sides, her toes no longer curled, her muscles no longer tensed. He continued the spanking, slowly but steadily easing the intensity until he was merely stroking the heated flesh of those perfect globes.

Zoë didn't move or react in any way. She lay limp and heavy over his lap and it occurred to him she might actually be asleep, a not uncommon result at the end of an intense session that culminates in full release.

I knew it, he thought exultantly.

He leaned over her, his mouth brushing the curve of her small, delicate ear. "You were born for this," he whispered.

She answered with a small, sweet sigh.

Chapter 4

Dylan's hands felt so good moving over her flesh. His fingers slid down along her ass to stroke the sensitive skin of her inner thighs. An extraordinary sense of peace and well-being suffused her, and she couldn't remember feeling this relaxed since she was a child. "Mmm," she heard herself murmur, a sound of pure satisfaction pulled from somewhere deep inside her. "Mmm."

She realized with a small shock that she couldn't move. Her bones had dissolved, and her muscles had turned to jelly. Finally she stopped thinking altogether and simply surrendered to the peace that enveloped her.

Strong arms suddenly lifted her into the air and set her down on the carpet. "On your knees, Zoë. Back straight, hands on your thighs."

It took Zoë a moment to return from the blissful place she'd been a moment before. She looked up to see Dylan standing over her, his hands on his hips. "What?" she blurted in confusion. "What's happening?"

Dylan was looking down at her, a half smile on his face. "I'm sorry, Zoë. I warned you the weekend would be intense. Normally I'd have given you more time to come down, but we only have so many hours, and I have a lot of things planned for you." He stood, and in spite of herself, Zoë's eyes were drawn to the very obvious erection tenting his shorts.

Her cunt spasmed in response, but when she looked again at his face, Dylan was frowning. "I gave you a direct command. Obey it at once."

Chagrined, Zoë struggled to replay in her mind what he'd said a moment before. Blowing out a breath, she scrambled to her knees. Dylan reached for a bottle of water he must have brought with him when he'd entered the room that morning.

He handed her the bottle. "You may drink as much of that as you wish," he said. "But pay attention because I'm only going to give you the next set of instructions once, and I expect you to adhere to them to the letter."

Whatever was left of the sensual lethargy she'd experienced while lying on his lap evaporated completely. He continued, "I'm going to go make some breakfast for us. While I'm gone, you will shower and groom. You may remove the collar while showering, but then put it back on. In addition to underarms and legs, you will shave your pussy and asshole completely smooth. There is a pair of barber's scissors in the drawer so you can trim before you shave, if you wish.

"Once you're done with grooming, you may dry yourself. You will not wear any makeup. You will pull your hair back in a ponytail. If you don't have an elastic in your bag, you'll find an unopened packet of them in the drawer as well.

"When I return, I expect to find you standing at attention beneath the suspension beam. I will inspect you carefully, so make sure you do a thorough job." He paused a beat. "Any questions?"

You bet your ass I have questions. Who the hell do you

think you are, telling me to shave my pussy and asshole? First of all, my asshole isn't hairy, thank you, and second, I'm here for a weekend. We're talking a matter of hours. How dare you order me to alter my appearance to such a degree? What's on the schedule after breakfast? You going to tell me to shave my head?

He was staring down at her, his eyes boring into hers, his mouth set in a firm line, power emanating from him like a force-field. She experienced a sudden crazy impulse to lean forward and kiss the top of his bare foot. What the hell was happening to her?

"No, Sir," she found herself replying.

Once he had gone, it was as if she'd been released from a spell. Unscrewing the cap of the plastic bottle, she drank deeply, nearly finishing the water in one gulp. It was refreshing, but what she really needed was coffee. A habitually early riser, she would have had two cups by now, and her body was pissed off that it hadn't yet had its quota of caffeine.

She hauled herself to her feet, reaching back to massage her still-tender bottom as she made her way to the tiny, doorless bathroom. She turned on the water in the shower and faced the sink, regarding herself in the mirror. Her cheeks and throat were flushed, the skin on her chest mottled as if she'd had an orgasm.

The experience had been more sensual than sexual, in spite of the pain, or perhaps partially because of it. She twisted back to regard her ass in the mirror. The skin was dark red and hot to the touch, a faint hint of bruising on her left cheek. A part of her was deeply shocked by this visual, but another part was drawn to it like a moth to a flame.

Turning back to face the mirror, she touched the red dog collar at her throat. No question—it had been humiliating when he'd attached that leash and led her by it to the basement. At the same time it had been exciting—a concrete testament of her new, if temporary, status as slave girl.

The room was filling with steam, recalling her to her task. She reached back behind her head, lifting her heavy hair to get at the Velcro closure. She pulled it open and slid the collar from her neck, placing it on the small counter beside the sink.

Reaching into the drawer, she found the small pair of very sharp scissors. She gripped a pubic curl between her fingers and carefully snipped it away, dropping the bit of hair into the small trashcan beside the toilet. When she'd trimmed as much as she could, she climbed into the shower stall.

As she stood beneath the hot spray, she pondered the morning's events. She'd been frightened at the prospect of the spanking, and had started out gritting her teeth, determined to bear it and get through as best she could. She had held her breath, tensed her body and squeezed her eyes shut in fearful anticipation. As the spanking had intensified, it was like being caught in a series of rough waves at the seashore—each wave nearly drowning her before she could catch and hold her breath for the next one. There came a moment when she nearly gave up, where she almost screamed out the safeword they'd agreed upon.

Yet somehow Dylan's deep, soothing voice had penetrated the panic, and the steadying comfort of his other hand on her lower back kept her anchored amid the torrent. Though it hadn't been a conscious decision, suddenly, instead of fighting the waves, she dove headlong into them. But rather than being sucked completely under, she found herself buoyed up to a place of serenity the likes of which she'd never experienced.

It wasn't that he'd stopped spanking her. If anything, he was hitting her harder than a moment before. But the stinging pain shifted into something different. Not pleasure, but something more encompassing and somehow loftier than mere pleasure.

Her hair washed and conditioned, she reached for the bar of creamy soap, lathering it over her body. She smoothed the sharp razor beneath her arms, following its path with the fingers of her other hand to assure she was completely smooth. There was a small, unopened bottle of baby oil she hadn't noticed her first time in the shower, and she used this to shave her legs.

She stared down at her trimmed pubic hair, and again the audacity of the man ordering her to shave her privates assailed her. At the same time, she couldn't deny the thrumming pulse of desire that emanated from her cunt and radiated outward like fire moving through her blood.

She moved the razor carefully over her sex, using both baby oil and soap to lubricate the blades' path over her skin. Just in case, she spread her legs and arched forward, drawing the razor between her ass cheeks. "I can't believe I'm actually doing this," she muttered aloud, as she stroked the now-smooth skin with her fingertips, in search of any errant stubble.

Most of the erotic romance novels she read were more vanilla than spice, but there was one novel in particular she'd read over and over, in which the Dom had shaved his sub girl while she perched on a stool, reaching back behind her to grip the legs of her perch for balance. The guy had purposely aroused his slave girl while he trimmed and shaved her pussy. She had to remain still, even when his fingers moved tantalizingly over her clit and swollen labia. Something about the mix of pleasure and danger—the possibility the Dom might cut his sub if she jerked suddenly—sent a jolt to some secret part of Zoë, a part that until last night she had always dismissed as not worthy of a strong, independent woman.

Turning off the shower, she reached for the towel Dylan had dried her with earlier that morning. Bending over, she twisted it around her head and stood, the terrycloth turban in place. She reached for the second towel and wrapped it around her body as she stepped out of the stall.

Rummaging in her overnight bag, Zoë retrieved her birth control pills. Pressing out the day's dose, she swallowed it with the last of the water in the bottle he'd given her. She removed the towel from her head and draped it over the towel rack.

She combed out her wet hair and tucked it behind her ears. Reaching for the collar, she secured it once more around her throat, making it a little tighter than Dylan had done the night before. As odd as it was to admit, she quite liked its snug feel around her neck. No—*like* wasn't the right word. It was as if the collar belonged there—as if without even knowing it, she'd been somehow bare without it—not her body so much as her soul. She looped a finger through the O-ring, thinking about its purpose.

She took the packet of thick, black elastic hair ties from the drawer. As she pulled her hair back and twisted an elastic into place behind her head, the second towel fell from her body.

Her eyes were drawn to her shaved pubis. She touched the area, running her fingers over the newly denuded flesh. Her clit gave a pulsing throb as she imagined standing at attention in the other room beneath Dylan's scrutiny.

She briefly considered masturbating just to take the edge off, Dylan's assertion that her body belonged to him for the weekend notwithstanding, but realized she had no idea when he might return. She didn't want to still be fumbling around in the bathroom when he came back to the room.

She made it into position just in time. As the deadbolt turned, she laced her fingers behind her head and arched her back, keenly aware of how this made her breasts thrust prominently forward. She spread her legs to shoulder-width, and felt a faint stir of air over her bare mons.

Using his shoulder against the door, Dylan entered the room with a large serving tray in his hands. The smell of bacon and fresh coffee assailed her nostrils, and Zoë had to swallow to keep from choking on the saliva that filled her mouth. Dylan did something on the side of the large tray that caused an attached metal stand to be released. He set the tray carefully on its stand near Zoë, and she saw a large plate heaped with scrambled eggs and half a dozen pieces of crisp bacon. Two large white ceramic mugs of coffee steamed beside the plate, one with cream, and one black.

They'd shared many cups of coffee while putting together their merger deal, and Zoë was gratified to see Dylan remembered she took hers black. The rich aroma of the brewed coffee beans was nearly too much for her. She had to forcibly restrain herself from falling out of position so she could grab the mug and take a long, restorative drink.

Dylan added insult to injury by picking up his mug and sipping it as he regarded her, his eyes lingering on her pubis before slowly moving to her face. "Nice," he finally said, taking another sip while her coffee cooled on the TV tray.

A tiny mewl of frustration pushed itself past her lips. Dylan smiled. "Is there a problem, Zoë?"

"Coffee," she muttered, and then remembered to add, "Sir. May I please have some coffee?"

"You may."

Dylan set his mug on the tray and reached for hers. Zoë started to reach gratefully for it, but was stopped by his sharp command. "Remain in position. I did not tell you to move out of position."

"But," Zoë began, confused. "You said—"

"I said you may have some coffee. I will hold the mug for you. You will remain in position."

Frustration, annoyance and need for the caffeine warred inside her, along with, if she were completely honest, another feeling—a strange, visceral thrill to be subjected to such complete and total control.

"Yes, Sir," she finally said, her eyes fixed on the coffee.

Dylan held the mug to her lips. The ceramic rim was cool, but the coffee was still hot. He tipped it carefully, and she sucked greedily at the strong brew. It was delicious. He let her sip for several long, lovely seconds before withdrawing the mug.

Turning back to the tray, he selected a piece of bacon and

held it close to her mouth. "Hungry?"

The caffeine had kick-started her appetite. "Ravenous...Sir," she said, her stomach growling in accompanying agreement.

Dylan smiled again, and held the meat to her lips. Zoë bit it and chewed, thinking nothing had ever tasted so good. He allowed her to eat the entire piece, and followed it with more coffee. He ate a piece himself, and then scooped up a forkful of scrambled eggs, cooked slightly wet, just the way she liked them. An explosion of buttery pleasure filled her mouth as she took the offered food. More coffee, more bacon, more eggs, until at last Zoë shook her head, her tummy full.

Dylan finished what was left on the plate, and then sipped from his mug, once more silently regarding her. She stared back at him, both confused and aroused. No one had fed her in her memory, though she assumed her mother must have when she was a small child.

Certainly she had never had to stand at attention, hands behind her head, butt-naked and shaved smooth, while the man who had just spanked her ass fed her bacon and eggs. If someone had told her just a day before she would be in this position, she would have scoffed and laughed, dismissing the prospect as not only absurd, but as demeaning to her as a woman and a person. Yet she felt anything but demeaned. She felt sexy, exotic, and as if she were perched on the edge of something both dangerous and exhilarating.

Dylan lifted the tray with its now empty plate and mugs and set it alongside the wall by the door. Returning to Zoë, he said, "Time for inspection." He stood close to her, so close her inclination was either to kiss him or to step back. She did neither.

He ran his fingers lightly under her arms and she giggled a little, instinctively pulling away. "Remain still and quiet," Dylan said, his voice calm but firm. Zoë stiffened and bit her lip in her effort to comply.

Mercifully he stopped tickling her, moving his hands down her sides as if sculpting her form with his touch. He crouched in front of her, his face only inches from her body. "Arch your hips forward and spread your legs wider," he commanded. "Show me that cunt."

A wave of heat washed over Zoë's face, but she forced herself to comply. Six million dollars, she reminded the part of her brain that still resisted what was happening.

To her dismay, Dylan reached into his shorts pocket and brought out a small flashlight. Leaning closer, he flicked it on, directing the beam over her spread pussy. He ran his fingers lightly over her labia, moving in a tantalizing circle over and around her clit. She couldn't stop the groan of pure lust that emanated from the back of her throat as he pressed two thick fingers into her wetness.

"Control yourself," he said in the same calm but firm voice, no trace of emotion in his tone. Flustered and chagrined, she struggled to obey, using every ounce of willpower to keep her hips from thrusting lewdly forward to force his fingers deeper inside. Instead she focused on the burn in her arm muscles from holding the unaccustomed position for so long.

He withdrew his hand and held it up for her to see. The

heat in her face intensified as she saw evidence of her arousal glistening on his fingers. He brought his wet fingers to his nose, closed his eyes and inhaled as if smelling a bouquet of flowers, a look of pure rapture moving over his features.

Zoë glanced quickly away, not sure if he was making fun of her, fervently wishing the inspection were over. Out of the corner of her eye, she watched him walk back toward a tall bureau beside the whip rack. His back to her, he pulled open a draw. She couldn't see what he was doing, but when he turned around, she saw he had pulled a disposable surgical glove over his right hand. He returned to stand in front of her. Zoë swallowed hard as she took in the tube of lubricant he held in his other hand.

"Turn around, bend over and grab your ankles," he said. "I'm going to inspect your asshole."

Zoë didn't react right away. Her body had frozen in place. Six million dollars, she reminded herself. Dylan was regarding her with an amused expression, one eyebrow cocked, as if waiting, even expecting, her to refuse.

Accepting the silent challenge, Zoë dropped her arms, which tingled as the blood rushed back into them. Turning, she bent forward and gripped her ankles, glad he couldn't see her face, which was now on fire.

She jumped a little when his fingertip moved lightly along the cleft of her ass, but managed to keep hold of her ankles. His finger was withdrawn, but a moment later cold lubricant was smeared over her asshole. Stiffening, she gripped her ankles tighter.

He moved closer behind her, reaching around her bent body with one arm to steady her as he pushed his finger gently but insistently past the tight ring of muscle at her entrance. "You're very tight," he observed, his tone clinical. He pushed the finger deeper inside her. "Are you an anal virgin?"

"No…Sir," Zoë managed between clenched teeth.

"Good," he said cryptically.

His ungloved hand was curled around her hip to hold her in position. He slid it down between her legs, and when his fingers skimmed her labia, a shudder went through her loins and her legs felt suddenly weak.

With his hard body pressed against hers from behind, he pushed a second gooey, gloved finger into her ass, his other hand strumming over her cunt. She began to tremble against him, losing her grip on her ankles, held upright only by his strong arms.

"Oh," she moaned. "Oh, oh, oh," the single syllable keeping time to his moving hands, which were turning her to liquid fire.

She was teetering on the edge of an orgasm, and desperate for the release. A welcome, dark twist of pleasure emanated from her core, and she groaned again, her body pulsating to his perfect touch.

All at once, he let her go—the fingers withdrawn from her ass, his supporting arm falling away, his perfect touch yanked from her throbbing, sopping cunt.

She stumbled forward, her hands flying out as she struggled to keep upright. "What? Wait, why?" she cried, frustration at the aborted climax rising like bile in her throat. She whirled around to face Dylan.

He was calmly pulling the lubricated glove from his fingers. He met her wild stare with a calm, amused gaze. "You nearly came, didn't you, Zoë?"

Well, duh.

"Why did you stop? I was so close!" The words tumbled out before she could stop them.

His look darkened, the half smile falling away. Zoë brought her arms around her torso, chagrined and confused. Her cunt was pulsing with need, her limbs trembling. She wanted to hit him. She wanted to scream. Damn it, she wanted to come!

"You forgot one of the rules, Zoë. That body is mine for the weekend, not yours. You are not to come unless or until I give you explicit permission. You're lucky I stopped when I did, little girl. If you'd gone all the way without asking, I would have had to punish you." He shook his head. "Clearly, you have very little self-control. One of the goals of a properly trained submissive is to control her own impulses—to subvert her immediate gratification in deference to her Master's wishes."

Several retorts rose to Zoë's lips, but she bit them back. Dylan was watching her. "What?" he said. "You have permission to speak freely for the moment. Tell me what just went through your mind."

Zoë pushed through the jumble of confusing emotions that were making it hard to think clearly. She wasn't used to being so off-balance with a man. She had always prided herself on being the one in control, both professionally and personally. Damn

Dylan Hart—since last night she had felt like she was walking through a fun house, the floor of her confidence tipping crazily beneath her feet, the walls of her experience at odd angles with what she thought she knew. "I'm not a submissive," she insisted, though the words rang hollow in her own ears. "I'm here as part of a deal, an agreement, nothing more."

Dylan regarded her silently for several beats. She stared back at him defiantly. "Nothing more?" he finally said in a quiet voice. When Zoë didn't respond, he continued, "So you're telling me you're here strictly to fulfill the terms of a financial obligation? Your reaction to the spanking, your reaction just now to the inspection—these were, what? Just you being polite?"

He lifted his fingers to his nose, his eyes fixed on her face as he made a show of inhaling the scent of her arousal. Zoë looked away, embarrassed and confused. Dylan's voice was low and hypnotic, and though she kept her head averted, she found herself hanging on every word. "So the idea of being suspended from that beam overhead—your wrists cuffed and secured, forced onto tiptoe by the tight pull of the rope and leather—holds no allure for you? You're indifferent to the possibility of standing naked and bound, unable to anticipate or avoid the next stroke of my whip?"

Zoë forgot to breathe.

Dylan moved closer. He reached for her shoulders, forcing her to face him. He stared down into her eyes. "I accept that you're here under unusual conditions, Zoë. I agree you entered into this agreement without full understanding of what I can offer you, or what I plan to take. But to say you're not submissive, to pretend you're here only to fulfill an obligation in order to further your career..." He trailed off, and dipped his head toward hers.

Taking her face in his hands, he touched his lips to hers. His kiss was light at first, but became more insistent, his tongue teasing along her lower lip and sliding into her mouth. He brought his arms around her. She could feel his cock like an iron bar between them as he pulled her close against his body. Her arms came up of their own accord and snaked around his neck as she kissed him back.

This was more like it! He was going to make love to her at last. She leaned heavily against him, silently willing him to move toward the narrow twin bed so they could fall upon it together.

As if reading her mind and obeying her unspoken command, Dylan cupped his palms beneath her ass and lifted her into the air. She locked her legs around his waist and buried her face in his neck. But instead of carrying her across the room, after a moment he lifted her away from his body and set her on her feet.

"Enough sweetness," he said, his voice gruff, his eyes glittering. He hooked his finger through the O-ring of her collar and pulled on it, forcing her up on her toes. "I told you this was boot camp, and time's a wastin'."

He let go of the collar and stepped back. Going over to the wall, he retrieved two coils of rope and a pair of leather wrists cuffs. There was a small stepstool leaning against one side of the bureau. He brought this, along with the rope and cuffs, back to where Zoë was standing.

Without saying a word, he opened the stepstool and

placed the cuffs and one of the rope coils on it. He unspooled the second coil, tying a slipknot at each end. He did the same with the second piece of rope. Zoë watched him, saying nothing, her mind temporarily short-circuited by thwarted sexual frustration and an undeniable fascination with what he was doing.

He reached for the cuffs and attached one to each rope, using a spring clip to secure them. He ascended the stepstool and looped the ropes over the eyehooks, pulling the knots tight. Stepping down from the stool, he moved it aside.

The ropes swayed on either side of Zoë, the leather cuffs dangling at their ends. "Lift your arms over your head," Dylan instructed in a quiet but firm voice.

Zoë stared up at the ropes, and then glanced anxiously toward the whip rack, her heart beating high and fast in her throat. "I'm not sure I—" she began.

Dylan cut her off. "It's okay, Zoë. You don't have to be sure. I'm sure, and I promise you this, I won't give you more than you can handle."

He reached then for her cheek, stroking it with two fingers, the gesture at once tender and extremely erotic. Zoë couldn't control the small tremor of lust, or was it fear, that moved through her frame.

"Now," he said softly. "Do as you're told."

Chapter 5

Dylan's balls ached. When he'd had her in his arms, her strong legs wrapped around his waist, why hadn't he just carried her to the bed, thrown her down and fucked her? It was beyond clear she wanted it as much as he did, so what was stopping him? After all, it wasn't as if he were her trainer. But he knew the reason, even as his cock demanded an answer.

Zoë Stamos was sexually submissive at her core, and every minute they had spent together since the night before only confirmed it more solidly in his mind. Beyond that, he sensed her sexual masochism, and the sensual sadist in him responded with a fiery rush of passion the likes of which he hadn't experienced in many years.

She was worth more than just a quick roll in the hay. She deserved all the energy and skill he could bring to their brief time together as Master and slave. His greedy cock would just have to wait to plunge itself into her tight, wet heat, not only until she earned it, but until he did as well.

Zoë lifted her arms, her eyes fixed anxiously on his face. He closed the soft leather cuffs around each wrist, which raised her arms high, but not high enough to suit him. Dylan mounted the stool and adjusted the ropes until she was forced up, not on her toes, which would be too tiring, but rather on the balls of her feet, her heels barely touching the carpet, her body stretched taut by the ropes.

He stepped back to admire the pretty picture, stroking his

cock briefly to calm its insistent call for attention. Her small pink tongue made an appearance on her lower lip, the gesture so sensual he nearly lunged for her then and there. She gripped the rope tightly in each hand above her cuffs. He could see the slight tracery of her ribs beneath her high, round breasts, and her bare pussy pouted at him as if begging for a kiss. She was watching him with those liquid dark eyes.

His cooler head prevailing, he selected a large, heavy flogger from the whip rack for her introduction to the erotic, intense stimulation that awaited her. He also chose a large plastic hair clip from the supply bureau.

Returning to the bound woman, he tucked the flogger in the back of his shorts and then twisted Zoë's thick, shiny hair up onto her head, securing it with the clip. He stepped back so she could see him, and took the flogger once more into his hands, allowing the luxurious suede tresses to glide between his fingers.

He held the flogger close to her face so she could smell the intoxicating scent of leather. "Kiss the whip," he commanded, "as a gesture of your willingness to suffer its lash."

"Oh," she said softly, a shudder moving through her. Beneath her fear, he could sense the burning need. He touched the whip to her lips, and her eyes closed as she softly kissed the handle.

Pleased, Dylan moved behind her. "We'll start slowly. I want to get a sense of what you can handle. The key here is to relax. Don't tense, don't anticipate. Don't let fear control your experience. Embrace the sensations, and let them take you where they will."

He brushed the flogger against her ass. "I'm scared," she blurted, forgetting the "Sir."

He didn't correct her. "It's okay to be scared. Use that fear. Channel it into strength."

"I don't understand."

"You will."

He swished the tresses over her back and shoulders, and graced the backs of her thighs with their leather kiss. For the next several minutes, he warmed her skin, acquainting her with the feel of the flogger against her flesh. When he gauged she was ready, he delivered the first real stroke, catching both ass cheeks simultaneously. He loved the way the dark leather contrasted to the pale skin and the slight jiggle of supple flesh beneath its stroke.

Zoë gasped, her shoulders tensing forward.

"Relax," Dylan reminded her. "Accept what is given to you."

He struck her ass again, a little harder than before. Again she gasped and jerked. He continued to flog her luscious bottom until she stopped gasping with each stroke, her hands finally relaxing their chokehold on the ropes.

Encouraged, he let a blow land between her shoulder blades, though he modified the stroke to allow for less padding beneath the skin, and thus greater sensitivity. Again came the small, startled gasp, and her fingers tightened once more around the ropes. Dylan kept his focus on her shoulders and upper back until the skin turned pink, and her fear subsided into something more manageable.

Stepping to the side, he drew back his arm and let the flogger fall hard against her ass, the blow pushing her slightly forward. She yelped, her breathy cry going straight to his cock. He delivered another stroke, just as hard, and then another. She began to dance on her toes in a vain effort to twist away from the lash, but Dylan easily followed her moves.

"Zoë, you're fighting the flogger. You're resisting."

"It hurts!" she cried, as he delivered a hot stroke to the backs of her thighs.

"It's meant to," he reminded her between lashes. "The pain is the entryway to where you need to go, to where you've always longed to go. Give in to it, Zoë. Let it wrap you in its arms."

He hit her harder. She twisted at the last second, which caused the tips of the flogger to wrap cruelly around her hip. Dylan, who believed in experiencing everything he gave to his subs, well knew how painful those leather tips could be when slamming against bone with sonic speed. "Stay in position," he admonished. "Show me your grace."

He flogged her ass with rhythmic, steady blows. She was panting, small mewling whimpers pushed out between breaths. She was taking a pretty intense flogging, especially for her first time out, but Dylan sensed it wasn't yet time to stop.

As happened when he was doing it right, he could almost feel the strokes as if he were on the receiving end of the flogger. Her emotions—the fear, the desire, the passion, the need—were all moving over and through him as if they belonged to him. As a dominant friend had once said when trying to explain the sensation—it was like flying a kite in rough winds. She was the kite, and it was up to him to skillfully manage the spool and line, to not only keep her aloft, but to help her soar.

Her yelps and whimpers had subsided into deep, guttural moans, and her head had fallen forward on her chest. She was close, but not there yet. *A little more, a little harder—you can do it*, he rooted silently, not wanting to distract her with words.

He whipped her steadily, the flogger flying over her skin from thigh to shoulder and back again. He focused again on her ass, which was now a deep cherry red. She was a natural, already so close to that powerful, sacred place that some subs took years to find.

Suddenly she grunted and jerked, as if coming out of a dream, and he felt the serenity subside like a wave falling back from the shore. "No," she moaned. "No. I can't, I can't, I can't." She began to twist and dance again, fighting the flogger once more.

"It hurts, it hurts, it hurts!" she whined, her voice edging toward panic.

"Fuck," Dylan muttered in frustration, angry not at her, but at himself. He had pushed too hard, too fast. He had wanted this too much. He ached to continue, to force her through sheer will to let go, but he knew from long experience that the moment was gone. He needed to back off and let her recover.

Slowly, he eased the flogger's stroke until the leather was once again only brushing her skin. Zoë was sagging against her cuffs. He moved to face her. Her eyes were closed. She opened them when he touched the handle of the whip once more to her lips. "Kiss the whip to show your thanks," he ordered.

She obeyed.

Reaching up, he quickly released the clips that held her cuffs, catching her arms as they fell forward. She leaned heavily against him as he guided her toward her bed. Fantasies of making love to her while she was still cradled in the arms of a submissive flying experience receded with each step. He hadn't yet earned the privilege. He would just have to try harder.

~*~

Zoë lay on her stomach on the bed. Dylan sat beside her. His hands felt good as he massaged her hot, stinging skin with a soothing lotion. She'd been terrified at the thought of the flogging, even more scared than she'd been of the spanking. Ironically, the spanking hurt more. Or no, that wasn't precisely accurate. The spanking packed more of a wallop than the flogger—Dylan's hard palm crashing down again and again against her ass. The flogger had been more sensual, if that was the right word, the leather like a lover's kiss, at least at first.

Those initial gentle strokes had lulled her into a false sense of security, the slow buildup easing her into accepting more and more, until suddenly she slipped over the edge of pleasure into a stinging, biting pain that radiated from shoulder to thigh. She'd wanted to take it, to embrace it, as Dylan had urged, even though she wasn't really sure what he meant. She wanted to prove to him, and to herself, that she could do this—she could handle whatever he meted out.

She had a sense she'd been close to something more—something somehow profound, but whatever it was, it had slipped away. For the second time since she'd agreed to their bizarre arrangement, she'd nearly shouted out her safeword. He'd stopped literally within seconds of her opening her mouth. She sensed his disappointment, and this upset her more than she cared to admit.

I'll do better, she silently promised herself, and him, even as she wondered why it mattered.

"You did great, Zoë," Dylan said, making her wonder for a second if she'd actually spoken aloud. "You really are a natural, perhaps even more so than I suspected. In fact, if I hadn't been so eager and pushed you too fast, I do believe you might even have flown. You're really something, you know that?"

Warmth moved through her body at his praise, the feeling she'd somehow failed replaced with a sense of accomplishment and hope. "Thank you," she said, her mouth lifting into a smile. "I've read about that concept—flying. It's a kind of endorphin release, right? Like a runner's high."

"You've read about it, huh?" Dylan countered. "So you know a bit more about BDSM than you've led me to believe?"

Zoë's face heated. She was glad he couldn't see her blush. "Well, yeah, I guess so," she admitted. "I mean, it's just fiction. I like to read erotic romances and sometimes they lean a little toward bondage and stuff like that."

She was relieved when Dylan didn't press the issue. "Flying," he elaborated, "*is* kind of a like a runner's high, physiologically speaking, but there's so much more to it. How do I explain it?" He paused, no doubt gathering his thoughts, and then continued. "I've heard it described by subs as a descent into fire and then a rising into the heavens. I know that sounds rather vague, but it does seem to be the process—moving through something really difficult and intense into something sublime. Maybe it's like a rocket when it's burning its way through the atmosphere and then the sudden break into outer space—into this vast, profound place of utter peace. As a Dom, when I'm truly connected to what's going on, I feel transported along with the sub into a kind of altered state, and the experience is truly breathtaking."

"It sounds amazing," Zoë said, a surge of longing moving through her.

"It is," Dylan replied softly. "And you shall have it." He released the hairclip and tugged at the elastic, pulling her hair gently free of its ponytail. He shifted his focus to her shoulders, massaging away the last vestiges of tension she didn't know she was still carrying. "I promise."

She must have fallen asleep, because when she opened her eyes, Dylan was still there, but a tray with a glass and a plate of cookies had magically appeared beside her. Dylan smiled at her. "You dozed off. I decided to get you some refreshment."

He lifted the glass from the tray. "I know you take your hot coffee black, and I also know you like your caffeine," he grinned, "but I want you properly hydrated for the rest of the day's events, so I decided to make you a nice big glass of iced coffee instead. I added a little sugar and a touch of cream. If you don't like it, I'll get you some water." He handed her the glass.

Zoë lifted herself to a sitting position as she eyed the cold drink skeptically. She was thirsty, and she reached for the glass. "Thank you." She never took sugar in her coffee, not because she didn't like it, but because of a lifetime of watching her weight and denying herself anything that might add unnecessary calories to her diet. And milk just plain made her gag. She avoided it at all costs. But Dylan was watching her expectantly, clearly pleased with himself, and she had to admit she quite enjoyed the novel experience of having someone wait on her.

Closing her eyes, prepared to find the coffee nauseatingly sweet and disgustingly milky, she sipped. She sipped again, and then took a big gulp. The coffee was strong, lightly sweetened, and stunningly delicious, the cream taking off that slight bitter edge that coffee always left on the back of her tongue. "That's good...Sir," she enthused, suddenly aware she'd forgotten to use the appellation during the flogging.

"Glad you like it. Have a cookie." Dylan reached for the plate and handed her a fat golden-brown cookie dusted with powdered sugar. Though she'd eaten a much larger breakfast than she was accustomed to only a while before, her mouth watered in eager anticipation.

Carbs, sugar, fat—cookies never featured in Zoë's regime, but neither did spending the weekend in a BDSM dungeon, so what the hell, why not? It smelled wonderful—the aromas of ginger, butter and molasses taking her back to childhood. Zoë bit into the soft, chewy cookie. "Mmm," she moaned, her mouth still full of cookie. "This is so good." It had to be homemade. "Did you bake this?" She couldn't stop eating it.

"Me?" Dylan shook his head with a laugh. "I wish I could take the credit, but no, my housekeeper, Adrianna, made them.

She's always trying to fatten me up. When she leaves for the weekend, she's prepared enough meals, cookies and cakes to feed an army. I usually end up taking most of the treats to work just to get them out of the house."

Zoë finished the cookie and greedily gobbled the second one as well, surreptitiously eying the plate to see if somehow she'd missed a third one. She resisted the urge to press the few remaining crumbs on the plate with her finger, and instead finished the delicious iced coffee.

Dylan stood and took the empty glass from her. He placed it on the tray beside the plate, and set the tray on the floor against the wall. Looking down at Zoë, he said, "Okay, break is over. Time for the next exercise. Do you need to use the bathroom?"

As soon as he said it, she realized she had to pee, and she nodded. "Yes, Sir."

"Do you need to move your bowels?"

Zoë was embarrassed by such a direct and personal question. "Um, no...Sir. I just, uh, need to pee." She started to rise to head for the bathroom, but Dylan put a restraining hand on her shoulder.

"Stay where you are. Lie back down on the bed, face down. I have to get a few things."

Confused, Zoë did as she was told, curious as to what Dylan had up his sleeve. She watched him stride across the room toward the wall with the whips, rope and chain. He stopped in front of the tall bureau and pulled open a lower drawer.

He returned to the bed carrying a small serving tray on which he'd placed several items. He sat beside her, placing the tray at the foot of the mattress. He picked up one of a series of what appeared to be oddly shaped dildos. It tapered to a rounded point not much bigger than a finger, widening along its length to a flared base. It was wrapped in clear plastic. He held it closer for her inspection. "Do you know what this is?"

Zoë swallowed, pretty sure from her reading that she knew what it was, but not wanting to hazard a guess. "I'm not exactly sure."

"It's called an anal plug. This is the smallest size, so we'll start with this one." He held up two others, each bigger than the last. Zoë stared in horror, and instinctively reached back to cover her bottom with her hands.

Dylan smiled, though his gold-flecked eyes were hooded. "Don't cover yourself, Zoë. A trained sub would be punished for that."

Zoë forced herself to lower her arms to her sides. Her heart was beating fast. Though she'd had anal sex with a few boyfriends in order to please them, it wasn't her favorite activity. "What?" Dylan said, cocking his head. "Tell me what you're thinking as you look at these plugs. Don't hold back. I want to know exactly what's going through your mind right now."

Zoë stared back, wondering if he *really* wanted to know the many, many things tumbling through her brain at that moment, nary a submissive thought among them. He regarded her with a somber, intent gaze. Okay, why not? He'd asked for it. So damn it, she would tell him.

"I'm thinking I most emphatically do *not* like foreign objects stuck inside me. I'm wondering how you'd like it if I shoved some hard piece of rubber up your ass, especially when you had to pee like a racehorse. I'm curious what kind of power trip you're on, to think I'll just go along with this. I'm wondering if this weekend is worth the six million after all."

As she spoke, his mouth quirked into a smile, which, by the time she was done, had spread into a broad grin. She knew she had gone too far, but it felt good to just get it out there. After all, he had asked.

"You done?" he asked, still grinning.

She lifted her chin. "Yes...Sir," she finally remembered to add. She stiffened, waiting for the flash of anger, the hard words, the promised punishment.

Instead, to her surprise, he said in a calm voice, "Thank you, Zoë, for that honest reply." He placed a comforting hand on her back. "You should know as we move forward, when I ask you to tell me what you're thinking, I really mean it. And I will never be angry or punish you for sharing your feelings." How did the guy get into her head like that? It was unnerving.

He continued, "That said, I understand you're frightened at the thought of this thing"—he held up the smallest of the plugs once more—"being inserted in your ass. You're afraid it's going to hurt. You're afraid you will lose control. I get it that it's embarrassing, even humiliating, from your perspective at this moment."

"Yes," Zoë agreed, relieved he understood. Some things were just beyond the realm of reasonable expectation, their agreement notwithstanding. She was glad he got it. She would go pee, and they could move on to whatever diabolical "exercise" was next on his list.

She started to lift herself on her elbows, but Dylan's hand stayed firmly on her back. "I didn't tell you to get up," he said. "Stay as you are." He pressed her back down onto the bed.

Confused, Zoë didn't resist. Dylan pulled the plastic wrapper from the anal plug and reached for the tube of lubricant. "Wait—what?" she exclaimed, refusing to believe what seemed to be happening. "But I told you—"

"You expressed your feelings. And that's a good thing. I listened and took what you said into consideration. Now we move forward. Get up on your hands and knees and stick out that pretty ass. I would advise you to relax as much as possible. It'll hurt less that way."

Chapter 6

"That's it. Easy. Try not to tense your muscles. You're doing great." Dylan stroked Zoë's back with one hand as he gently pressed the tip of the smallest plug into her pert, sexy ass. He'd added enough lubricant to accommodate a bowling ball, but she still squealed and jerked forward as he pressed the flared end of the plug into her anal passage.

"All done," he informed her. "How does it feel?"

She twisted her head back to regard him, still in position on her hands and knees. "Full," she said. "Not as bad as I thought it would be. It only hurt at the last second going in." She appeared surprised by this. "I think it's okay now." She wrinkled her nose, adding, "But I really do have to pee."

"I know." Dylan pressed gently on the flat rubber circle that peeked between her cheeks. "Think of it as erotic discomfort, with emphasis on the erotic aspect. You're suffering for me because it pleases me. Do you understand that?"

"Not really...Sir."

Dylan smiled. "That's okay. You will." He patted her ass. "Now, I'm going to remove this plug and put in a larger one. This next one is a vibrating plug. You might find it more, uh, interesting."

Zoë gave an exasperated sigh, grounds for punishment in a properly trained slave, but forgivable in the circumstances. She had already exceeded all his expectations for the weekend, and it was only the first day. Her potential was enormous, and he couldn't wait to continue their exploration.

Zoë's head was still twisted back to regard him as he spoke. "I'm going to take out the smaller plug now," he said. "Removal is much easier than insertion. Stay relaxed and in position, head facing front." Her face was a study of mixed emotions, but finally she did as she was told.

Reaching for the plug, Dylan tugged gently, pulling it carefully from her tightly-muscled anus. Zoë sucked in her breath as it popped out. Dylan laid it carefully on the tray and selected the vibrating plug. He unwrapped the sterile packaging and squeezed a healthy dollop of lubricant over the plug's tip.

"Okay, time for the second plug," he informed his temporary slave girl. His cock was throbbing with some insistence in his shorts, but he forced himself to concentrate on his task. Taking his time, he pressed the hard rubber phallus carefully into Zoë's ass. This one slipped in much more easily, her anal muscles still relaxed from the first one. Nevertheless, she squealed and flinched when the flared base was pressed home. Dylan stroked her back soothingly. "All done. I told you, you're a natural." He depressed the small button at the base of the plug, and heard it whir to life inside her.

Zoë grunted, her body stiffening. "Flow with the sensation," Dylan advised. "The experience can be quite pleasurable, if you allow it to be."

"It—it tickles. It feels weird." She wriggled her ass provocatively, and it took every ounce of Dylan's self-control not to push her down then and there and thrust his rigid cock into her. "I really have to pee, Sir," she added petulantly. She was twitching and squirming like a little kid.

"That would be a bit messy," Dylan replied dryly, allowing himself a smile she couldn't see from her position. "Hopefully you can hold it a little longer. I have an exercise in mind for you first. Lie down on your back and draw up your legs, feet flat on the mattress, knees spread wide. I'm going to watch you make yourself come. As soon as you do that, you will be permitted to empty your bladder."

She stilled. "Wait, what? With this thing still in me?" She twisted back once more to regard him, her eyes flashing with something that bordered on defiance. "You want me to do what?"

"You didn't hear me?" Dylan countered, staring back at her. She didn't move or reply as they locked eyes. He counted slowly to five in his head, and then barked, "I gave you a direct command. Obey it at once!"

"But," she began plaintively.

"I didn't give you permission to speak," Dylan interrupted. "Do as you're told."

He continued to stare her down and finally, her face crumpling in defeat, she looked away. With obvious reluctance, she rolled to her side and then onto her back. Her face was rosy with embarrassment as she drew her legs toward her body and let her knees fall open to reveal her smooth, pouting cunt.

Dylan's mouth actually watered at the lovely sight and his cock, if it was possible, hardened even more. "Go on," he said softly. He reached into his shorts to stroke himself into a more comfortable position. "Make yourself come for me."

"Oh god," Zoë whispered, more to herself than to him, it seemed. She closed her eyes and lifted her right hand to her lips. She licked her fingers and placed them between her legs. Dylan could hear the muted whirring of the vibrating plug buried in her ass. Zoë began to rub the petals of her silky vulva with hesitant fingers.

"Open your eyes," Dylan commanded, his voice hoarse with lust. "Keep them focused on my face while you masturbate."

Her fingers stopped their tentative dance. She opened her eyes and fixed them on his. The color on her cheeks deepened and spread to her chest. Her lips were parted, her nipples engorged and erect.

"Go on," Dylan urged.

She began to rub herself again, this time with more conviction, her eyes locked on his. She slid a single finger inside herself and then drew it up over her vulva, slick with her own juices. She was sheer perfection, and Dylan found himself holding his breath as he watched her erotic gyrations. After a while she began to pant, her hips lifting slightly, her knees spread wide. "Oh, oh, oh," she cried, her eyes fluttering shut, her fingers flying, the scent of her arousal driving him mad with lust.

"Eyes open," he reminded her. He reached into his shorts and gripped his throbbing shaft, drawing his thumb over its lubricated tip. "Ask permission when you're ready to come."

She opened her eyes and stared directly into his soul, her

pupils fully dilated, her breath rasping in her throat. "Oh, oh, oh," she moaned again. "Oh god, oh fuck, oh please..." She began to shudder, her fingers twirling over her swollen, glistening sex.

"Ask," Dylan reminded.

"Please!" she gasped. "Let me come. May I come? Permission to come—oh!"

She was already coming, that much was clear, but he didn't want to introduce failure into the moment, and so he said quickly, "Yes. Come for me, Zoë. Give me all you have."

Her hips lifted from the bed, her head falling back, her body wracked with several powerful spasms. Finally she collapsed back against the mattress. Her skin was flushed and covered in a sheen of perspiration, her hair wild about her face, her chest heaving.

Dylan lay down next to her on the bed and rolled her gently to her side. "I'm going to take out the plug now. Stay still," he told her. He turned off the vibrator and tugged gently to remove the plug from her body. After the initial resistance, it slid out easily, and he dropped it on the tray beside the first for later sterilization.

He curled behind her and pulled her close against him. He held her for a long time, until the thudding of her heart eased, and her breathing slowed. "Are you asleep?" he whispered.

"No, Sir," she whispered back. "But I really need to—"

"I know." Dylan laughed and pulled away, sitting up. "You really need to pee. I'd say you earned the right. So hop up and let's go to the bathroom. We'll use the opportunity to further your submissive training. Have you ever peed standing up in front of someone else?"

He paused, watching with amusement as a look of horrified incredulity moved over her features. "I take it from your expression that's a no." He shrugged. "First time for everything."

~*~

Zoë wondered if she'd ever blushed as much in her entire life as she had since arriving in the home of Dylan Hart. Her face was once again on fire as she stood in the shower stall, legs planted on either side of the drain, desperately willing her uncooperative body to let go of what felt like a gallon of liquid pressing painfully against her bladder. Dylan watched her with that calm, implacable expression of his, a fire glowing just behind his eyes.

She was still weak from the powerful orgasm he'd given her, though it was her own hand that had done the work. Never in her life had she been both so controlled and so free—so tightly embraced in the cocoon of another's domination, and yet so filled with exhilaration and light, as if she might break free of gravity were it not for the comforting tether of Dylan's steadfast, assured mastery.

Whatever she'd been expecting this weekend, so far the experience couldn't be contained in any of the relationship compartments she'd created over the course of her life. Dylan had made her do things she never would have dreamed of doing on her own, yet each step of the way, she'd found herself fully involved and eager to continue, even when it frightened her a little. The man was like no one she'd ever met. While he was masterful, he wasn't a bully. And while he was tender and loving, there was an underlying quiet confidence and masculine assurance that was deeply appealing to a woman used to running the show.

"Come on," Dylan urged, snapping her back to the moment. "You have five more seconds. If you're not going to pee, we'll just continue with our next exercise."

This implied threat did its job. At last her body gave her a break, and a steady stream of hot urine splashed down between her legs. The relief was immediate and immense, even as she continued to blush. When she was done, Dylan reached for the detachable showerhead and turned on the water. He aimed the spray between her legs.

"It's cold!" Zoë yelped, twisting away.

"Builds character," Dylan replied with an evil grin. After a moment, he turned off the water. "Step out and assume an at-attention position, arms behind your head. I'll dry you."

Zoë did as ordered, experiencing a curious mix of embarrassment, comfort and erotic thrill as Dylan gently but thoroughly dried her legs, pussy and ass. She couldn't help but notice the sizable erection bulging in his shorts, and her self-consciousness evaporated as her body responded with a surge of desire.

Was she experiencing that remarkable thing she'd read of in so many romance novels—love at first sight?

No, that wasn't right, because they'd worked together on the financial venture, spending sometimes as much as sixteen hours a day in each other's presence, and while she'd found the man attractive and charming enough, there had been no longing, no ache of desire as she experienced now.

So was it, then, just what he offered? This heady mixture of dominance and tenderness, of passion and erotic "suffering" that had somehow captured her complete attention?

Whatever it was, she wanted Dylan Hart. She wanted him more than she'd ever wanted another man. And more to the immediate point, she wanted him inside her. She wanted him to take her, then and there, caveman style, right on the bathroom floor.

As seemed to have happened over and over since their meeting at the bar the night before, Dylan spoke now as if he had been privy to her secret thoughts. "I want you," he said in a low, urgent voice, his eyes hooding with an unmistakable look of lust.

"I want you...Sir," she replied, her voice breathy with desire.

Without further preamble, he reached for her and lifted her into his arms. He carried her from the bathroom to the small bed in the corner of the dungeon and laid her with surprising gentleness on the mattress. His eyes fixed on her face, he ripped his shorts from his body, revealing a large, thick cock that pointed toward her like a divining rod, a drop of pre-come balanced on its tip.

With a primal growl, he fell upon her, his heavy, masculine weight pinning her down as he reached for her wrists. He pulled her arms over her head, pressing them hard against the mattress on either side of her head as he dipped his head to kiss her.

His mouth was urgent over hers, his lips and tongue sending shivers of pleasure and need through her body as he kissed her with fierce passion. When he pulled away, she instinctively lifted her head, trying to follow his mouth and win it back, but he held her down by the wrists, and she fell back against the pillow.

His mouth blazed a trail of tingling heat along her throat toward her right breast. His lips closed over her nipple. Teeth and tongue worked in perfect tandem, at once teasing, suckling and biting, the pleasure and pain inextricably woven together in an explosion of sensation.

He released her wrists as he shifted his body lower, until he was perched between her legs, his breath hot on her skin. With strong, determined hands, he pressed her thighs apart and lowered his head. His tongue snaked out and stroked a line of wet heat along her labia. Zoë shuddered and moaned, wantonly lifting her hips in a silent plea for more, more, more.

His fingers were digging into her thighs as his thumbs held back her folds and his lips and tongue moved with exquisite skill over and around her spread cunt. It wasn't long before she began to shudder and buck against him, teetering precariously on the edge of yet another powerful orgasm. Her mouth was open, and she tried to get her lips to form words. She tried to get her voice to stop its breathy gasping so she could ask permission for the orgasm that was hurtling like a freight train directly toward her.

"Please," she finally managed to gasp. "Can I—"

But before she could get out another word, he was suddenly up and over her, his large hands once again closing around her wrists as he pulled her arms over her head. Lifting himself, he angled his body until the head of his cock was pressing insistently between her legs. Nearly faint with desire, she shifted beneath him so that her wet, aching cunt could receive him.

He groaned as he thrust himself almost savagely into her. If she hadn't been sopping wet, he might have hurt her. As it was, her body eagerly, even desperately, grasped for him, her vaginal muscles clamping down hard in spasm against his girth. He groaned again, and she moaned in reply. She lost herself in their lovers' dance, her busy mind finally shutting down as her body took over, all conscious thought spilling away like water tipped from a bowl.

When some semblance of coherence returned, Zoë opened her eyes to see Dylan, lifted on one elbow, smiling down at her. "I was about to initiate mouth to mouth, just to get you breathing again," he said with a smile. "You okay?"

Zoë stretched like a cat and sighed happily. "Better than okay, Sir." *Sir.* She had to admit, she quite liked the way the word tripped off her tongue.

"What?" Dylan said, watching her in that intense way he had. "Tell me what's going on in your head right now."

"I was thinking about trust," she said, amazed how easy it was to talk to him. All the shyness, hesitation and posturing was just—gone. "I was thinking I didn't really get this whole D/s thing before. I mean, I've read about it a little."

"A little...?" Dylan prompted with the lift of an eyebrow.

Zoë laughed. "Okay, okay. I'll admit it. A lot. It always seemed, I don't know, weird. This whole concept of erotic pain and sensual submission. I just didn't really get it. Or no, that's not right"—she paused, trying to figure out what she wanted to say—"I did understand it on an intellectual level, but I couldn't figure out how an independent, strong woman like me could possibly want to submit, sexually or otherwise, to a man. Even though the concept attracted me on some level, I didn't think it was something I could do, or should *want* to do, if you follow me."

Dylan nodded. "I do follow you. I experienced a similar confusion in my early twenties when I was first coming to grips with my own dominant impulses. I love and respect women, so why did it get me so hard to tie a woman down and whip her? To cane her ass, to see her tears, to watch her writhe in erotic pain? What the fuck was *wrong* with me?"

Zoë lifted herself on an elbow, too. "Wow, yeah, right? So, what's the answer, Mr. Hart? Are we just two sick puppies?"

Dylan laughed, shaking his head. "No. We're just hardwired a little differently than your average vanilla bear."

Zoë laughed at this, but sensed he had more to say. Dylan continued. "Here's what I figured out, with some help from trusted mentors I met along the way. In the end, it's about liberation. Women's liberation, men's liberation—just plain old human liberation. It's about being truly free to express who and what we are, not based on society's dictates of what we are *supposed* to be, but rather what really moves us—what reaches our hearts and minds, what allows us to connect with another person. It's a consensual exchange of power that elevates both of us—the Dom and the sub—to a higher plane of experience." He gave a small laugh, looking suddenly self-conscious. "I'm sorry, I tend to get on my soapbox about this. You just need to tell me to shut up."

"No, not at all," Zoë assured him. "The whole thing is fascinating. I mean, I thought when you made this bet it was just some elaborate way to get into my pants," she admitted with a grin.

Dylan laughed. "Well, there *was* that." Then he sobered, the smile falling away from his face. "Seriously, though, Zoë. There's something I have to tell you."

Zoë's stomach did an unpleasant twist. Was this where he admitted he had a girlfriend, or worse, a wife, stashed away somewhere? She held her breath, waiting.

"The money—it's already being transferred into your account."

It took Zoë a second to process this sudden change in topic from what she'd anticipated. "I'm sorry, what?"

"I want you to know that now. What's happening between us, it's not about some bargain of my investing in your venture in exchange for this weekend. I'm already sold on the business deal. It's done." When Zoë didn't respond, he continued, "What I'm saying is, you don't have to finish out the weekend—not on those terms." A shadow moved over his rugged face. "You're free to go. I don't want to keep you here as part of a some deal."

Zoë stared at Dylan, trying to understand, a sudden

coldness moving through her and making her shiver. Was he sending her away? "Do you want me to go?" she said in a small voice, tears pricking her eyes.

Dylan smiled tenderly and reached for her. "No. I want you to stay. What I'm trying to say is, I want you to stay, but not because you have to. I want you to stay because you want to."

His smile, his words, his touch, all combined in a burst of sunshine to warm her from the inside out. She realized with a sudden shock that the business deal she'd been working so hard to put together, and with which she'd been consumed for several months, hadn't even entered her mind since Dylan's proposal the night before.

"I want to," she said with conviction. "Please, Sir. I want to stay."

Chapter 7

Zoë wasn't used to sleeping during the day. She woke slowly, taking a moment to get her bearings. They had eaten lunch on Dylan's back veranda, which overlooked a beautifully tended lawn that sloped toward a small lake. Afterward, he'd suggested a nap, but instead of taking her back to her dungeon bed, he'd led her to his bedroom on the second floor.

From the moment he'd told her their financial bargain was no longer in play, something had shifted between them. What Zoë had started out regarding as a weekend kinky sex game had become something infinitely more real.

Refreshed from the afternoon nap, Zoë gently disengaged from Dylan's warm embrace, stretched and yawned. Dylan opened his eyes and smiled sleepily at her. He took her hand and guided it to his cock, which lay long and thick along his flat stomach.

"Now that you're rested," he said, "we'll continue with the next exercise." His smile was lazily sensual, his shaft twitching against her fingers.

Zoë's cunt spasmed, her nipples perking to instant attention. Certain she knew what he wanted, and eager to give it to him, she started to scoot down to take his erection into her mouth. He stopped her by gripping a handful of her hair and using it as a rein to jerk her back. "Not so fast. You're making assumptions. I would prefer it if you wait until I give you a specific task, understood?"

Both embarrassed and chagrined, Zoë nodded.

"What's that?" Dylan prompted.

"Yes, Sir," she managed, secretly thrilled at his dominance, which resonated somewhere deep inside her, filling a place she'd never realized was empty.

Dylan slid from the bed and stood beside it, completely relaxed in his nudity as he placed his hands on his hips, his cock jutting provocatively toward her. He pointed to the ground. "Get on your knees."

He waited while she obeyed. His shaft bobbed inches from her face. She swallowed and pressed her lips together, only barely controlling her impulse to lean forward and suck that gorgeous cock into her mouth. "Hands behind your back," he instructed. "Grip your opposite wrists with your hands." Once she was in position, he continued, "You will worship my cock with your mouth. You won't stop until I climax." His tone was matter-of-fact. "I think we'll make this more interesting with a little rope. Oh, and do you know what nipple clamps are?"

No point in denying it. "I've—I've read about them in my novels, Sir," Zoë admitted.

"Ah yes, your erotic romance novels." Dylan lifted an eyebrow, his smile sardonic. "You're going to have to show me some of those later, sub girl. But right now, it's time to experience what you've only read about." He reached back and opened his nightstand drawer. He pulled out a chain with an alligator clip attached on each end. He held it out so Zoë could see. He pressed open one of the clips and indicated the small screw at its base. "You understand the principle, I assume?"

Zoë's stared at the open clip, fixating on the double row of tiny, sharp teeth glittering like a shark's open maw. It looked positively diabolical. "Yes, Sir," she whispered. "I—I think so."

"Allow me to demonstrate." Dylan bent down and reached for Zoë's right nipple, pulling it taut between his fingers.

"Oh!" Zoë gasped, instinctively drawing back in alarm. "Will it hurt?"

Dylan's smile was at once sensual and cruel. "Of course it will hurt. That's the point, dear heart." He rolled her marble-hard nipple between thumb and forefinger. "But it's a *good* pain. It's purifying. And it's part of this exercise—you will please me while at the same time suffering for me, which in turn pleases me all the more."

As Zoë pondered this dichotomy, Dylan opened one of the clips and guided it toward her distended nipple. "Don't move. I'm going to attach the clips one at a time, and then we'll adjust the tension, okay?"

"I'm afraid," Zoë blurted, her body tensing, her heart pounding.

"That's okay," Dylan replied. "Part of the process is working through your fear. You're safe, Zoë. I promise. Remember, you're the one in ultimate control here. If you feel you have to stop the action, just use your safeword. Remind me what your safeword is."

"Buyout," Zoë whispered.

"Buyout," Dylan repeated with a nod. He still held her nipple in a tight grip. "Now, take a deep breath and release it slowly while I count. At three, I'll put the clip on your nipple. It hurts the most at first, and then it kind of numbs. It's nothing you can't handle, I promise. These are the gentlest kind of clamps because we can adjust the tension."

An involuntary shudder moved through Zoë's frame, despite his reassurances. "Deep breath," Dylan reminded her, and Zoë took in a big lungful of air, letting it out slowly as Dylan counted. "One...two...three."

She gasped and instinctively jerked back as the clip bit down on either side of her engorged nipple. A sudden explosion of pain ripped through her nerve endings, and tears sprang unbidden to her eyes. But, as Dylan had promised, after a few seconds, the tension was tolerable, dulling into something manageable. Then came the second clip, and a second explosion. Zoë blinked back a fresh rush of tears.

Dylan tugged gently at the chain between the two clips. "I think that's just about right," he said. "We won't go tighter for now."

Thank god for small favors. She watched in silence as he took a small hank of white rope from the nightstand drawer. He knelt behind her, his erection pressing briefly against her ass as he wrapped the rope snugly but gently around her wrists. The knowledge that he was as aroused as she was pleased her. Being bound made her feel both more vulnerable and more excited. Her cunt was throbbing, her mouth watering with desire to taste his beautiful cock. Her nipples pulsed in the tight grip of the clamps and she prayed she'd be able to make him come without the use of her hands, and with the distraction of the clamps and rope.

Finally satisfied with her bonds, Dylan returned to stand in front of her, his cock once more inches from her face. She leaned forward, her lips parting of their own accord. He took a step back. "Don't move," he said. "I will control this, not you." He placed his hand on her head, moving it over the top and back, his fingers curling to grip a handful of her hair.

He pushed her head slowly forward until the tip of his cock brushed her lips. "Take my offering," he said, his voice deep and commanding. He slid his shaft into her mouth until the head touched the back of her throat.

Zoë gagged a little, struggling to accommodate his sizable girth, determined to show him she was accomplished at least in this. He kept his cock in that position for several long seconds while she willed herself to relax and accept it. Finally he withdrew it slowly, letting its silky weight glide sensually in her mouth. She closed her lips and suckled along the length to create friction as he moved. He groaned softly in what sounded to her like deep satisfaction.

Pleased and emboldened by his reaction, she teased along the underside of his cock with her tongue as he eased himself back into her mouth. He brought his second hand to her head, letting go of her hair with the other, and using both to guide her onto and off his shaft in a pumping rhythm that became faster and faster as he neared climax. It wasn't long before he gave a deep, guttural cry and stiffened. She could feel the hot, sudden spurts of his jism sliding down the back of her throat, but could do nothing except try to swallow so she wouldn't choke.

Finally he let go of her head and moved back until his cock slid from her mouth. He dropped to his knees and drew her into his arms, his hands sliding beneath her bottom. Standing, he lifted her and set her gently on the mattress on her side.

The mattress gave as he sat beside her, and then the ropes were plucked from her wrists. He rolled her gently onto her back. He was still breathing heavily from his orgasm and his eyes were bright.

He placed his fingers on either clip over her compressed, now nearly numb nipples. A look of genuine regret moved over his features. "There's something I didn't mention before. Taking off the clamps is the worst part. The bad news is, it will hurt like a motherfucker. The good news is, it'll be over in a flash."

He was right, on both counts.

They washed together in Dylan's huge walk-in shower. Dylan had Zoë dry his hard, masculine body, and then he dried hers, his touch incredibly sensual. As he worked, he said, "I was thinking we should go out to dinner tonight. I know the perfect place." There was something teasing in his tone, and his eyes were dancing.

Zoë kept her tone light as she teased back. "Oh, yes? And where would that be? A BDSM dungeon?"

Dylan's mouth quirked into a half smile, his eyes sparking with a fire that sent a jolt of electricity through Zoë's core. "Precisely," he agreed. "How did you guess?"

Zoë's gut clenched. "Wait, what? I was just kidding."

"Well, you hit it on the head nevertheless. The club I belong to has a very fine private restaurant, along with two fully equipped dungeons and even accommodations for out of town guests. Saturdays are always hopping, and it's the best night to show you the ropes." He grinned, adding, "No pun intended." Zoë's return smile was faint, her mind still trying to process what he was saying.

"The club's in Larchmont. It's actually an old hotel a couple of guys in the scene bought," Dylan continued. "I spend a lot of my free time there. I'm one of the staff trainers, though just on a part-time basis, since obviously investment banking takes up most of my time. I'd love to take you to dinner, and then we could check out the dungeons. We can watch a few scenes, meet a few folks."

Zoë thought about this. She imagined the kind of place this BDSM club must be, with whips and chains on the walls, and people dressed in leather and thigh-high boots. "What would I wear? I didn't bring anything but the clothes I arrived in."

"Do you have a black cocktail dress and black heels at your apartment?"

Zoë nodded. "Of course."

"We'll stop by your place, then, and you can change."

~*~

"Master Dylan, a pleasure to see you, Sir. Two for dinner?" Sara, one of The Vault's staff slaves, smiled at Dylan. He glanced at Zoë, who stood beside him looking a little flustered and a lot gorgeous in her slinky black dress, red slave collar and fuck-me high heels. Zoë's eyes were on Sara, who wore the staff slave uniform of a black leather collar with matching cuffs around her wrists and ankles, her only other clothing a satin thong of the skimpiest variety. She was a pretty girl, save for skin pitted with acne scars. Her hair was long and very blond, her body slender. Silver barbells pierced both nipples, with a matching piercing in her belly button.

"Yes, Sara. Thank you." Sara led them into the small but pleasantly appointed dining room of the converted hotel. There were three other couples already seated, some eating dinner, some sipping glasses of wine, heads close in conversation. Mistress Sylvia, an imposing Dominatrix dressed in a full-length black gown, sat at a table. Her partner, Gene, knelt on the floor beside her, wearing nothing but a cock cage locked around his privates, his mouth open as his Mistress fed him from a large piece of chocolate cake.

"Oh," Zoë murmured softly as they passed the couple. Dylan was holding her hand, and he gave it a reassuring squeeze. In the short time they'd spent together, Zoë was teaching him to see the beauty and intensity of D/s with fresh eyes. Tonight would be another facet of that experience. Aware the scene could sometimes be a little overwhelming, he made a silent promise to assure her introduction was a positive one.

Sara led them to a table close to the large archway that opened into the main dungeon. Dylan pulled out the chair that gave Zoë an unobstructed view of the action. He sat across from her and ordered a bottle of wine. Once Sara had gone, he put his hand over Zoë's. She was staring through the archway, beyond which several scenes were already in play. At his touch, she turned to look at Dylan, and he locked eyes with her, a rush of dominance surging through him like a hit of cocaine.

"I want to continue your training while we're here. Is that acceptable to you, Zoë?"

Her eyes widened, her hand moving up to touch her slave collar. "Yes, Sir," she breathed. He hadn't permitted her to wear a bra, and he could see the alluring curve of her nipples against the silky fabric of her dress.

"Excellent. Stand up and remove your panties. Place them on the table between us."

Zoë's eyes darted around the room. "Right here?" she whispered.

"Zoë," Dylan said, adding a note of sternness to his tone. "Do as you're told."

She swallowed visibly, but pushed her chair back from the table and stood. Again glancing nervously around the room, she reached beneath her clinging dress and dragged her panties down her slender, bare legs. She dropped a hand to the table for balance as she stepped out of the underwear. Her face flushing a rosy hue, she set the bit of silk and lace on the table as instructed.

Sara approached at that moment with a bottle of Cabernet and two glasses. If she noticed the panties lying in the center of the table, she gave no indication. She expertly uncorked the wine and poured a small amount in Dylan's glass. He tasted it, nodded to her and watched as she filled both glasses.

The restaurant had no menu, but offered three specials each night. Sara recited them and Dylan chose the Porterhouse steak with sautéed mushrooms. Zoë, still blushing, rallied enough to order the rosemary chicken with wild rice. When Sara had again retreated, Dylan said, "Tell me what you see beyond the archway. Describe the scenes to me." He kept his eyes on her face.

She licked her lips nervously. "There's a woman with her dress undone and hanging down at the waist," she said, speaking so softly Dylan had to lean forward to hear her. "She's got clamps on her nipples, except they look different than what you used on me." Zoë hugged herself, covering her breasts in what Dylan guessed was an unconscious gesture.

It had been incredibly hot when he'd tied Zoë's hands behind her back while she knelt naked on his bedroom floor waiting to receive his cock. Her sweet, breathy gasp of pain when he'd clipped the alligator clamps on her nipples had been music to his sadistic ears. Though he'd wanted to hold out for as long as possible, when her mouth closed over his cock, he was a goner, barely managing to hold back his orgasm for more than a few minutes before giving in to her incredibly sensual, skilled ministrations.

"Probably clover clamps," he suggested. "We'll try those when you've had a little more experience. They can be rather intense."

Zoë reached for her glass, looking adorably flustered as she sipped her wine.

"Go on," Dylan urged. "What else do you see?"

Zoë set down her glass and returned her focus to the dungeon. "There are two men, one on either side of her. She's bound to one of those X crosses. They're, um, they're whipping her breasts." Dylan could hear the whisper of leather against skin. Zoë hissed in sympathy, rocking slightly in her seat.

There was the distinctive sound of a woman's cry of pain,

and Zoë gasped, "Oh! One of the guys flicked her nipple and the clamp flew off." The woman screamed again. "Oh my god! He did it to the other one!" Zoë hugged herself tighter, her teeth worrying her lower lip, her eyes glued to the scene. "Okay, phew. They're removing the wrist cuffs. Oh, one of the guys is helping her off the cross. Aw, they're kissing and people are clapping." She looked at Dylan, flashing a relieved, beautiful smile in his direction.

Sara reappeared with two glasses of ice water, followed by Matt, another of the staff slaves, who carried a tray bearing their dinners. Matt, like Sara, was essentially naked, save for the black leather codpiece covering his package. Matt, who belonged to one of the club's owners, was tall and muscular, his body shaven smooth. He had lettering tattooed on either deltoid—*Hank's* on the right, *Boy Toy* on the left.

They set the food on the table. Sara refilled their glasses and inquired if Dylan needed anything further, still ignoring Zoë's black lacy panties resting on the white tablecloth. Dylan tucked into the delicious, perfectly cooked steak with gusto. Zoë, he noticed after a moment, was barely picking at her food. "Is it okay?" he asked solicitously. "If you don't like it, we can order something else."

"No, it's delicious," Zoë said hastily. She smiled shyly. "I don't know. I just don't seem to have much of an appetite right now. There's so much to take in."

Dylan nodded. "So there is. It's hard to remember that newness—that sense of discovery and awe when you first put your toe in the waters of a BDSM lifestyle. I'm jealous of you in a way—everything is shiny new and filled with potential."

He picked up her panties and brought them to his face, inhaling her sweet, delicate scent as she looked down at the table, obviously embarrassed. He tucked the panties under his thigh and reached across the small table to lift her chin. He looked into her eyes and said gently, "You don't need to be shy with me, Zoë. And you don't need to be shy here at The Vault. Everyone here *gets* it. This isn't a tourist club for gawkers who think it's trendy to pay a cover charge to get into some sleazy S&M theme club down in the city. This is a members-only safe place where people come together to explore and share their love of the lifestyle."

They watched in silence a moment as Sara preceded Master Tom, who was followed by his two slave girls, both of whom were completely naked, their legs chained together so they were forced to hobble in tandem behind him. Tom settled at a nearby table, the two women kneeling on the floor side-by-side next to him.

Zoë turned back to Dylan. "I have to say, I feel, I don't know"—she shrugged, her eyes sliding back to the threesome—"intrigued by all this, but kind of out of my ken. Everyone seems so relaxed, so comfortable." She waved her hand in a vague way around the room. "I don't know if I could ever get used to being so vulnerable, so *exposed*, in front of strangers like that."

Dylan stroked her soft cheek with two fingers. "First, let me say this. In the short time we've been together, you've pleased me tremendously. You should know, there's no right or wrong here, as long as you do your best and give of yourself with honesty and grace, which I believe you have done, and then some."

Zoë smiled at this praise. "Thank you, Sir," she said with

such simple submissive grace that Dylan's heart clutched hard in his chest.

"Answer me this," he said, forcing himself to keep his focus. "If on Friday morning someone had told you you'd spend the day in some guy's BDSM dungeon doing the things we did, and that not only would you handle it, but you'd *revel* in it, would you have believed them?"

Zoë laughed, shaking her head. "No way, José! I can barely believe it myself."

Dylan nodded. "Exactly my point. But here's the thing—you were open to the experience. You didn't shut down and close yourself off from your feelings or reactions. You gave it, and me, a chance. That's what we're doing tonight. I don't expect you to strip and walk into that dungeon and climb up on that cross. I don't plan to force you into anything you're not one hundred percent ready to do. It will be your call, Zoë."

"But I thought it was the Dom who was in charge?" Zoë queried.

"The Dom is in charge, yes, but ultimately it's the sub who calls the shots. It's that whole concept of a consensual exchange of power. As soon as you withdraw consent, on whatever level, for whatever reason, that's a game changer. Now, some folks get into it a little deeper—a Master/slave relationship might remove some of the consent, or rather, it's agreed upon that the slave gives up his or her right to refuse, but even then, it's a kind of fiction, if you will. The underlying consent of the basic tenets of the relationship still remains." He shrugged. "Who knows, you and I might eventually want the added intensity of a Master/slave connection, or we might not. But the bottom line is, it's about what *we* want, as a couple, same as in a vanilla relationship."

"Relationship?" A corner of Zoë's mouth quirked into a half smile. "I agreed to a weekend, but here we are talking about next week, next month…?"

Dylan swallowed hard, keenly aware how very much this mattered to him. What had started out as a kind of lark—a bet with himself regarding Zoë's submissive potential and his ability to expose and nurture it—had turned into something much more, and more quickly than he could have imagined. Several snappy retorts leaped into his brain, but he shook them away. Now wasn't the time to prove how clever he could be. He would lay it out there, and let the chips fall where they may.

He stared into Zoë's luminous, dark eyes. "I won't presume to speak for you, but I will tell you this—I'm thirty-three years old, Zoë. I've been in several serious relationships, though it's been a while since I put my heart out there. Like you, I work a lot of hours on the day job, but I'm coming to realize that isn't the be-all and end-all. I want to focus more on what really matters in my life."

He put his hand over hers. "I saw something in you and it spoke to me. I took a chance, but I never dreamed our connection would be so instant and so complete. I'm not saying we should get married tomorrow"—he gave a small, self-conscious laugh, but Zoë's intense, receptive expression gave him courage to continue—"but I want more than just to complete the terms of some bet, and I hope I'm not being presumptuous to think you want more, too. I guess what I'm saying is, yes—let's go crazy and use the R word."

Zoë said nothing for a long moment. Then she placed her second hand over his, the light pressure of her fingers sending warmth through his body. "Let's do," she said, an impish grin lighting her face. "Let's go crazy." Then she laughed. Dylan felt as if his heart had suddenly sprouted wings, and he laughed with her.

He pointed to her plate. "Maybe you want to eat a little something before we venture into the dungeon?"

She looked down at the untouched food on her plate and then back up at him as she reached for her fork. "Wow, I just realized I'm *starving*."

Chapter 8

After Sara cleared away the remains of their dinner, Dylan fixed Zoë with a dark, sexy look. "Shall we, sub girl?"

Zoë glanced through the archway to the dungeon beyond. "Yes, Sir," she whispered, pushing back her chair.

At the first scene station Dylan took her to, a naked man hung upside down by his ankles, his head only inches from the floor. While a second man secured the sub's wrists behind his back, a woman held a penis-shaped gag to his lips. He opened his mouth wide. She slid the phallus in and buckled the straps around his head.

The woman picked up a small wicker basket from the ground nearby and held it toward the male Dom. He reached in and took a handful of clothespins. She did likewise, and set the basket down again.

Several more people had gathered to watch the scene, all standing a respectful distance from the station, all silent. With quick, practiced hands, the pair attached clothespins to the suspended man's scrotum, penis and nipples, the wooden pins fanning out in tight circles. Zoë could almost feel the pinch as the spring-tightened tips closed over delicate flesh, but the bound, gagged man seemed to accept the torture with a calm stoicism.

Once they were satisfied with their handiwork, the pair each produced a short-handled single tail whip. Zoë drew in a sharp, sudden breath of shock when the male Dom flicked his whip in the direction of the clothespins ringing the sub's right nipple. One of the pins flew off, leaving a dark, angry mark in its place. The sub jerked in his restraints and issued a strangled cry of pain. Unable to control her reaction, Zoë found herself yelping softly along with him.

Dylan's arm came around her shoulders. "Remember," he whispered into her hair, "this is fully consensual." Zoë nodded, but leaned gratefully against him, unable to look away.

Standing on either side of their sub, the two Doms took turns snapping off the clothespins, one expert, agonizing flick at a time. As the man jerked in his bonds, his face red and contorted, Zoë whispered, "What if he needs to use his safeword?"

"Hand signals," Dylan whispered back. "If there's ever a time you can't speak, you agree on a hand signal or some other gesture to take the place of a safeword. When you're in a position with me where you can't speak, your silent safeword will be the opening and closing of your right fist." A thrill of nervous anticipation shivered through her at these words. He hadn't said *if* she was ever in a position with him where she couldn't speak, but rather *when*.

When the last clothespin was flicked away, the woman knelt beside the suspended man and removed the gag. She stroked his face gently with a small cloth as the other Dom used a kind of pulley mechanism to lower the man to the ground.

Dylan and Zoë moved to another scene station, this one containing a large woman dressed in a tight satin dress, bound on her back to an inversion table and tilted so her head was lower than her legs. Three men were clustered around her, their cocks fisted in their hands, taking turns thrusting their erect shafts into her open mouth.

Dylan, his arm still around Zoë, led her past that station toward an ajar door at the back of the dungeon. "This second dungeon is for more intense scenes," Dylan murmured as they crossed the threshold. The lighting in the second dungeon had a red cast to it, creating an eerie atmosphere. A half-dozen people were standing quietly along the wall, four men and two women, all of them facing the center of the room.

Zoë followed their collective gazes and her mouth fell open in shock as she took in the scene before them. A slight woman with large, dark eyes and a shaved head was suspended by chains that hung from the ceiling, shackled to her wrists. Her slender, naked form was pulled taut by her bonds, her feet forced up on tiptoe. A large, shirtless man in jeans, his torso covered in tattoos, was carefully inserting long, thin needles in a circular pattern around each of her nipples. Thin lines of blood ran down the girl's breasts from some of the insertions, droplets splattering to the plastic mat on which she stood.

At the sight of the bright red blood, Zoë felt suddenly woozy and a little sick. She buried her face in Dylan's chest. "Hey, it's okay," he said softly, stroking her hair. Zoë took several deep breaths, reminding herself of Dylan's previous words: This is all consensual.

"Look at her face, Zoë," Dylan urged quietly. "Tell me what you see."

Steeling herself, Zoë forced herself to look again, this time focusing on the girl's face. The sub was staring at her Dom with what could only be called adoration, her eyes shining, her lips softly parted, no evidence of pain or suffering in her features.

"Pain is a very subjective thing," Dylan added, his voice close to Zoë's ear. "Erotic suffering can be transcendent, in the right circumstances."

They watched for another long minute, until Dylan whispered, "Had enough?" to which Zoë gratefully nodded that she had.

They returned to the dining room, where Dylan introduced Zoë to Hank and Michael, the owners of The Vault, along with a few other people sitting at the long bar that ran the length of the room. They engaged in casual small talk, as if the scenes, involving whips, chains and even blood, going on beyond the archway were the most normal thing in the world.

For this particular venue, Zoë supposed, they were. Both exhilarated and exhausted, she was eager to leave when Dylan made their farewells and led her to his car in the parking lot behind the converted hotel. On the drive home from the club, Zoë's mind was teeming with images and thoughts about what she had witnessed that night.

She was glad Dylan wasn't compelled to make idle conversation. He seemed comfortable with the silence as he focused on the road. It was as if he instinctively understood she needed to time and space to process the events of the evening, and her reaction to them.

As they undressed and prepared for bed, Zoë couldn't resist stealing glances at Dylan's muscular, broad frame. Had it been a typical relationship with the usual sort of guy she had found herself with over the years, she wouldn't have hesitated to make it abundantly clear she was ready and willing for a little pre-sleep sex.

With Dylan, however, she found herself content to wait for his signal. He was the one in charge, and as odd as it was to admit to herself, she found she quite liked it that way.

When they lay down together, her mind and body were still thrumming with sexual excitement from the evening's adventures, and she doubted she would be able to fall asleep very quickly, not with this sexy, naked man holding her against his warm, hard body.

Yet she must have fallen asleep, her rest deep and dreamless, because when next she opened her eyes, the sky outside the window was the pearly gray of predawn. Dylan was awake beside her, his hands moving sensually over her body. She lay still, savoring his touch on her breasts, her belly, her thighs.

When he finally rose over her, nudging her thighs apart, she was more than ready to receive him. Wrapping her arms around his back, she pulled him down, a guttural moan of pure lust wrenched from somewhere deep inside her. They made love for hours, by turns rough and gentle, finally stopped only by sheer exhaustion.

The next time Zoë opened her eyes, the room was flooded with sunshine, the sound of birds twittering outside the windows, and for several sleep-fogged seconds she had no idea where she was. There was no undercurrent of steady traffic punctuated by the beep and clang of garbage trucks and the angry honks of impatient drivers. The bed was impossibly comfortable, one of those mattresses that mold perfectly to the body, and the sheets were soft and cool against her bare skin.

Dylan was still asleep, a sexy five-o'clock shadow whiskering his strong jaw. He was on his back, the sheets pushed down to reveal his muscular, smooth torso and, as her eye trailed down the lines of his body, she saw the tip of his cock peeking just above the sheets, its erect outline visible beneath.

Zoë scooted silently down on the mattress until her face was level with Dylan's hip. She lifted the sheet and leaned over his erection, tenderly cradling his balls in her hand as she closed her mouth over the head of his cock.

At first he didn't move or react, his breathing deep and even. Zoë took her time as she glided her tongue down the length of his shaft to take him fully into her mouth. She lifted her head and lowered it again, creating a gentle friction with her lips as she moved.

She was startled by his hand, which suddenly closed over the back of her head, his fingers curling into her hair as he held her down. He pushed gently but insistently until she was fully impaled on his shaft, her nose pressed to his pubic bone. Her heart began a rapid tattoo against her sternum, her windpipe blocked by the way his cock was lodged in her throat. Panic began to edge its way through her system when she tried to lift her head to breathe, and his large, strong hand prevented her from moving even a fraction of an inch.

Her lungs began to burn, and there was an uncomfortable pressure building in her head. Was it happening already—was he purposely putting her in a position where she couldn't speak, and would need to use her signed safeword? Her right hand was caught beneath her side, her left hand still curled around his balls. Would the left hand count? Could he even see it?

She pushed again against his firm hand, trying to lift her head, managing to gurgle a sound of distress. All at once he let go, and she fell back against the bed, propelled by the force of her movement.

Gratefully she sucked in air, not sure if she was angry, or excited, or both. Before she could sort out her feelings, Dylan was on top of her, his fingers closing tightly around her wrists, which he jerked hard over her head as he shifted between her legs, forcing her thighs apart.

As before, she was soaking wet, her cunt greedily sucking him in and clamping down. He thrust hard inside her as he lowered his mouth to hers and kissed her, long and deep. Then he nuzzled against her neck, while he continued to thrust in and out, his cock stroking a sweet spot inside her, the sensation rapidly building into something she knew she couldn't control for long.

"You belong to me, Zoë. You understand that now, right?" His voice was a low, sexy growl, his words punctuated with those perfect strokes that were rapidly sending her toward orgasm from the inside out.

"Yes," she managed to gasp from beneath his masculine weight. "I understand, Sir."

"That means you're mine to do with as I will," he continued. "This weekend is only the beginning. I will take you further than you ever dreamed possible. I will possess you completely and thoroughly. You will submit in every way to me. You will suffer for me, and you will experience exquisite pleasure, the likes of which you never knew existed."

He swiveled his hips as he continued to thrust, and Zoë felt the climax rising like a wave, ready to crash at any moment. "Do you agree, Zoë? Do you freely give yourself to me, mind, body and soul?" He lowered his head and bit her right nipple, his hips and cock doing something extraordinary to her body, his hands still tight around her wrists.

The small explosion of pain at her nipple only fueled the lust already boiling over inside her. Was her submission freely given? Or was there in fact no choice in the matter? However she might intellectualize her response or her feelings, her entire being was shouting yes! Any remaining choice had been removed by a desire so powerful it obscured any other possibility. She was already enslaved, the word *no* erased from her vocabulary.

"Yes!" she finally managed to gasp, just before the climax robbed her of language or coherent thought. "Yes, yes, oooh, yes…"

~*~

"New sub infatuation," Louis said knowingly. "Based on past experience, I predict you'll be over her by the end of the week."

Louis Sutton was Dylan's oldest friend in the scene, and the one who had sponsored his membership at The Vault. They'd met at a bondage workshop Louis had put on for a BDSM group

Dylan had been loosely affiliated with when he had lived in the city. Louis was older by a good twenty years, but they'd always enjoyed each other's company. Though they crossed paths regularly at The Vault, they made it a priority to meet up for a beer from time to time after work.

"No," Dylan protested, shaking his head. "This is different. Our connection was instant and multi-faceted. She's amazing, Louis. She's new to the scene, but the most trainable, passionate submissive I've ever been with. This is it. She could be the one."

"Well, then, I'll call Jill right away. She'll want to get started on the wedding preparations." Louis laughed. "You've known this girl how long now?"

"Well, just a few weeks, but—"

"You've been involved for a few weeks and you're ready to pop the question? Who are you, and what did you do with the real Dylan Hart?"

"Well, no," Dylan admitted, aware he was weakening, rather than strengthening his case. "We haven't actually been involved for a few weeks. We worked together on a business deal. But this past Friday we got together—involved, as you say." Dylan decided not to tell the older man just how that involvement had started.

"So, wait," Louis said with exaggerated slowness. "Let me make sure I have this straight. You're telling me you spent a weekend with this girl, with this newbie to the scene, and based on those few hours, you've determined she's the most trainable, passionate submissive you've ever met?" The skepticism dripped from his words.

Dylan shrugged, his grin sheepish. "Look, I know it sounds weird, but what can I say? You haven't met Zoë. I'm telling you, this girl is one in a million."

Louis grinned and shrugged back. "Hey, I'm sure you believe what you're saying right now, and I really hope for your sake it's true. After all, as Jill never tires of reminding you, it's well past time you settled down, boy."

While Dylan had had relationships over the years, and been in love a time or two, he had never met a woman he could imagine growing old with, and saw no reason to settle just because he was over thirty. Louis and his wife/sub, Jill, had married in their early twenties, and, soon after they met Dylan, Jill had made it her personal mission to find Dylan his ideal mate. Dylan had gone along for a while, but it had never worked out, and finally he'd forbidden her from trying.

Louis took a long pull from his beer bottle and held up the empty in the direction of an approaching waitress. He nodded toward Dylan. "Want another?"

"No, thanks," Dylan said. "I have some work I have to get done tonight."

"Not seeing Ms. Right? How will you survive?" Louis teased.

"Regretfully, no. She's closing a big deal in the morning, and we agreed it was best if she stayed at her place."

In fact, Zoë had said it would be best, and Dylan had pretended to agree, when what he'd really wanted to do was insist she drop everything in her life and commit herself fully, twenty-four/seven, to whatever was developing between them. Still, he recognized she was being the mature one in the matter, and in point of fact, he, too, had plenty on his work plate, including a venture capital deal that might necessitate a trip down to Washington, DC later in week, though he was hoping Ed would be able to handle the meeting on his own.

The waitress set a fresh bottle of beer in front of Louis and cleared away their empties. Louis glanced at his watch, picked up his bottle and drained nearly half of it in one gulp. He set down the bottle and wiped his mouth with the back of his hand. "Okay, so when do we get to meet this model of submissive perfection?"

Dylan laughed. "Hey, I didn't say she was perfect—she's a work in progress, like all of us. That's half the fun, right? She's eager, sincere and full of potential. When I brought her to The Vault on Saturday, she was like a kid in toy store, just taking it all in."

"Hey, Jill and I will be at the club this Friday. Maybe you two can join us? Hank's got some bigwig whip maker visiting from Australia. He's going to demonstrate some of his wares on some lucky sub and Jill, pain slut that she is, has already volunteered to be his victim, er, subject."

Dylan nodded. "I'd heard something about that. It would be fun for Zoë and me to pick out a whip together."

Louis whistled, shaking his head. "Already picking out whips. I better tell Jill to put a rush on those wedding invitations."

"Uh huh," Dylan replied sarcastically.

"Seriously, though," Louis continued, "We could meet for dinner and a little dungeon action. You know Jill—she'll immediately take Zoë under her wing and show her the ropes." Louis chuckled at his pun.

Dylan nodded thoughtfully. The idea of bringing Zoë into the fold was appealing. It made their fledgling relationship that much more real. Jill was a good egg, and a good friend for Zoë to have in the scene. She made it a personal mission to welcome all submissive newbies, both male and female, into The Vault. She'd even organized a submissive support group through the club.

Louis set down his empty bottle, reached into his pocket and dropped a twenty on the table. "Seven o'clock work for you?"

"That sounds perfect. I'll check with Zoë and let you know."

~*~

"Hi, Daddy." Zoë clutched her phone in excitement. Finally she'd done something all on her own, something big, and even Anton Phillip Stamos III wouldn't be able to poke holes in this one.

"Zoë. I'll get your mother."

"No, wait. I called to talk to you."

There was a beat, and then, "Is everything all right, young lady?" His tone made her suddenly feel sixteen again, her heart in her mouth as she tried to figure out a way to tell her father she'd backed her new car into a pole.

Shaking away the feeling, she said brightly, "Everything's fine, Daddy. Better than fine. I just brokered my first solo deal. A ten million dollar capital venture funding for a small tech firm."

"What do they sell?"

"Nothing yet. But they're on the cusp of developing the technology that's going to revolutionize mobile battery life. The money is to continue the research and development."

"Sounds awfully vague. Risky, too."

"There's some risk, certainly," Zoë admitted, managing to keep her voice calm and level. "The risk is defined and assessed, and the funds are priced accordingly."

"What are the terms? What stage of development has the company's product reached? What is the current and projected valuation and performance in terms of sales, earnings and dividends?"

Zoë, who could recite this information in her sleep, after having lived and breathed the deal for months, began to discuss the specifics of the deal. It felt good to finally have her dad treat her as an equal.

Her father listened, harrumphed, and then launched into more questions, peppering them at Zoë as if she were on a witness stand, accused of murder. "To what extent have their budget and projections been substantiated? What's the pre-money versus the post-money valuation? What's your fee? What are the pro-rata rights?"

A headache began to bloom behind Zoë's eyes as she tried to explain and defend a deal she'd felt until this phone call to be iron clad.

When she finally sputtered to a frustrated halt, her father intoned, "I don't know, Zoë. It doesn't sound to me as if you've really thought this through completely. Your brother would never take this kind of risk."

And there it was.

Anton Phillip Stamos IV—the exalted can-do-no-wrong son who went from Wharton School of Business directly to Goldman Sachs, and earned more in a year than she had earned in a decade. *He* wouldn't have structured the deal this way. *He* wouldn't even have considered it. Therefore, it must be bad.

"Can't you just say congratulations?" She heard the whine in her voice, and silently cursed herself.

Her father cleared his throat. "Congratulations, Zoë," he said, his tone formal. "I only hope you don't come to regret it."

"Thanks, Dad. I really appreciate your support," she said, not bothering to hide the sarcasm. "Is Mom there?"

When she'd hung up with her mom, Zoë laughed to herself. What the hell had she expected? Just because *she* was different, what made her think her father would have changed?

And then it hit her with the force of a physical blow. She didn't need his approval to be happy. She had done something big, something that mattered, and it wasn't just about making money—she had helped secure funding for a company she really believed in, and she had done it on her own. Yes, it was a risk, but what was life without risk?

She picked up her phone again. She wanted to talk to Dylan. She wanted to see him. She wanted him to share her joy. She could trust Dylan Hart. In the brief time they'd spent together, he'd proven that again and again.

She typed out a quick text. *Hi. I miss you.*

Almost instantly, her phone buzzed in response and the words scrolled across her screen. *Me too. I'm at my office pretending to work, but all I seem to be able to do lately is think of you. I'm so glad you texted. I was going insane "giving you space".*

A smile split Zoë's face. *You're in the city?*

Yep. I could be there in fifteen. Then you won't have to miss me anymore.

Yes, please, Sir.

Chapter 9

"Wow," Zoë enthused, looking at herself in the three-way mirror of the small, upscale BDSM boutique dressing room. "It's gorgeous, though now I get why Victorian women were always fainting." Madam Lucy, the proprietress, had spent fifteen minutes lacing Zoë into the impossibly tight but otherwise surprisingly comfortable crimson leather corset. Zoë's figure was compressed at the waist by restrictive bone stays, her breasts forced up like two plump peaches, the bodice of the corset cut so low the tops of her nipples were showing.

Zoë was mildly embarrassed to be so scantily and sexily clad in front of a stranger, but Madam Lucy was wearing something equally revealing—a low-cut outfit that clung to her voluptuous and obviously naked form beneath the sheer, lacy gown. The boutique was by appointment only, and Dylan had clearly been there before, as Madam Lucy greeted him with such effusive affection it would have made Zoë jealous, if Lucy weren't old enough to be Dylan's mother.

Dylan's eyes moved hungrily over Zoë's body, the approval clear in his expression. "It will be perfect for your debut tomorrow night at The Vault."

"My...what?" Zoë asked faintly, tottering suddenly on matching red stiletto heels Madam Lucy had added to the ensemble. When Dylan had said he wanted to get her something sexy in celebration of the successful funding of her tech company, she'd imagined some lingerie to be enjoyed in the privacy of Dylan's bedroom and dungeon. The sudden awareness he planned for her to wear this skimpy thing in public cast the outfit in a new light. She twisted back to regard Dylan directly, her arms crossing protectively over her nearly bare breasts.

"My good friends, Louis and Jill Sutton, will be there," Dylan said. "We can join them for dinner, and then there's going to be a demonstration by this Australian whip guy. Jill has volunteered to be his subject. She's what Louis fondly calls a pain slut—she can take quite an intense whipping. It's really something to see."

The devious smile lifting Dylan's lips belied his casual tone. "Then I thought it might be fun for us to engage in a scene of our own. Nothing too intense—a little light bondage, maybe a flogging—just a taste of public submission to give you a more, uh, personal experience of the club scene."

Zoë turned back to the mirror, regarding herself with this new information in mind. The thought of a public scene engendered what was becoming a familiar conflict of emotions since she'd stepped into Dylan Hart's dungeon—fear and desire balanced on either side of the D/s scale.

Dylan came up behind her and wrapped his arms around her, resting his chin lightly on her shoulder as he stared into the reflection of her eyes in the mirror. "It's not a request," he said softly, though she could feel the quiet power beneath his words. "It's my desire to offer the gift of your submission to my friends in the scene. That would please me, sub girl. Would it please you?"

She could feel his erection hard against her lower back as

he held her. He dipped his head and brushed the bare skin of her shoulder with his lips, his arms tight around her.

And just like that, the scale tipped.

"Yes, Sir," she said with conviction, though her heart was fluttering like a bird. "It would please me."

~*~

Zoë twisted back her head to look at Dylan as he removed the wrap from her shoulders. Her dark eyes were wide with both trepidation and anticipation. He smiled encouragingly, hoping she was as proud of herself as he was of her. She was stunning in the dark red leather corset, which molded perfectly to her slender but curvaceous form. Her silky stockings rose to mid-thigh, revealing swaths of tan, smooth skin just waiting to be marked with a whip. He'd permitted panties, though he silently reserved the right to remove them during their planned scene—he hadn't yet decided.

They'd continued her submissive training during the course of the week, both stealing as much time as they could from their day jobs, neither worrying overmuch about sleep or lack thereof. Dylan was looking forward to the weekend, during which he planned to turn off his cell phone and computer, and insist she do the same.

As Jenna, a staff slave who served as hostess when Sara wasn't available, led them into the dining room, Dylan spied Louis and Jill, both of whom were waving in their direction. Dylan made the introductions. Jill, a statuesque blonde, reached to take Zoë's hands in hers. "What a pleasure to meet you, Zoë. You're even lovelier than Dylan claimed." Jill's smile was warm and sincere, and Zoë smiled back, visibly relaxing as she settled into her chair.

Wine was ordered and poured, and entrees chosen. Small talk about careers ensued for a few minutes and then Jill, predictably, turned the conversation to the upcoming whip demonstration. "Louis has volunteered me for the main scene," she said confidingly to Zoë. "This guy they have visiting from Australia, Master Cameron, he's like one of the premier whip makers in the world! I've heard through the grapevine he's a stern taskmaster—very old school 'slaves should be seen and not heard' intense." She wrapped her arms over her small breasts, which were visible beneath the sheer, silvery fabric of the clinging, sleeveless dress she wore, and shuddered dramatically. "I'm so nervous I could pop!"

Dylan met Louis' eye at this proclamation. Louis grinned conspiratorially. Jill never missed a chance to scene at the club, and the more public the venue, the better.

Zoë asked, "How long have you been coming to The Vault?"

"Since its inception, about eight years ago." Jill glanced at her husband. "Right, Louis?"

Louis nodded. "Yep. We're founding members. One of the owners, Michael Nowicki, and I go way back. We met in med school and discovered our shared fetish for all things BDSM quite by accident when we ran into each other at one of those sleazy underground clubs that used to proliferate in the city back in the pre-AIDs days. Michael had a dream all the way back then to create a safe, clean, welcoming environment for folks like us, but, as he says, life got in the way for a decade or two."

As if summoned by the conversation, Michael, a short, wiry guy with curly gray hair and smiling blue eyes, approached their table. "Hey, buddy!" he exclaimed, clapping Louis on the back. "Nice to see you and your lovely bride." Turning to Jill, he added, "You ready to get up on the stage and give us a good show tonight, slave girl? I hear Master Cameron's brought a dragon tail just for the occasion."

"Oooooh," Jill breathed, bringing her hands to her face, her round, hazel eyes opening wide with pretended fear that didn't hide the lust just beneath it. She glanced around the dining room. "Where is this famous Master we've heard so much about?"

"He's back in the lounge setting up his gear for sale," Michael said. "I hope you guys brought your wallets. His stuff ain't cheap." He grinned, his gaze turning now to Dylan and Zoë. "Good evening, Dylan. A pleasure to see you again, Zoë." His eyes moved appreciatively over Zoë's corseted form. "I hope we get to see *more* of you tonight—perhaps at a scene station, hmm?"

Zoë looked down at the table, her cheeks flushing slightly, and then glanced at Dylan. He smiled, placing his hand on her arm and giving it a gentle squeeze as he addressed Michael. "That's the plan. My sub girl is ready and eager to make her scene debut at The Vault, aren't you, Zoë?"

Zoë swallowed, drew in a breath and lifted her chin in that charming way she had when mustering her courage. "Yes, Sir," she said, her voice low but clear.

~*~

A large space had been cleared on one side of the main dungeon and folding chairs were set in rows in front of a portable stage erected against the wall. Shortly after the meal was over, Jill had left the dining room to meet Master Cameron and discuss the scene. Apparently this guy was a big deal, as every seat was already occupied, with more people standing in groups behind and around the limited seating area. They sat in the front row, Zoë between Louis and Dylan.

Hank was on the stage with Matt. They were setting up a steel frame X cross toward the center back of the stage. There was a long folding table nearby with several ominous looking black leather whips laid out one alongside the other.

The preparations apparently completed, Matt stepped down the small set of stairs to the right of the stage while Hank moved forward toward a microphone stand. He tapped the live mic and the room immediately quieted. "Good evening, fellow perverts," he said, his words greeted with laughter and a smattering of applause. "Tonight we have a real treat in store for you. Master Cameron of whip making fame has flown across the world to personally demonstrate a new line of bullwhips and dragon tails he's created for serious players in the scene. Master Louis has graciously offered the services of his slave girl, Jill, to serve as the subject, or rather, the object, of Master Cameron's considerable skills."

Hank glanced to the side of the stage and Zoë, following his gaze, saw Jill standing there, alongside a tall, broad-shouldered man with long, dark hair pulled back in a ponytail, his chiseled features movie-star handsome. The BDSM uniform she'd come to expect at the club—black leather pants and vest with no shirt beneath—molded perfectly to his muscular form. He radiated power and authority, as if he were Master not only of the woman beside him, but of everyone in the room, Zoë included.

"Without further ado, I introduce Master Cameron." Hank held out his hand in a welcoming gesture.

Master Cameron took the steps in one leap and was on the stage, Jill trailing behind him. He faced the audience, flashing a brilliant white smile that set off his extremely blue eyes. "G'day mates," he said, "it's a privilege and an honor to be here tonight." There was applause, and he inclined his head slightly, the gesture almost royal. Finally he turned to Jill, who was standing beside him, smiling broadly.

"Hank and Michael have asked me to do a little demonstration to get things started. This lovely sub girl has graciously volunteered her considerable"—he raked her body brazenly with his eyes—"talents to assist me." Speaking directly to her, he added in a peremptory tone, "Strip and present yourself at the cross, back to the audience."

Jill at once peeled out of her clinging dress, though she left on her black stiletto heels. Her pubic hair had been shaved and shaped into a small heart just above her cleft, and two hoops of gold glittered on her labia as she moved. Her breasts were small and high, the dark pink nipples elongated like eraser tips at the end of new pencils. She curtsied prettily toward Master Cameron and then sashayed gracefully to the X cross.

Master Cameron followed her. His body obscured hers as he cuffed her wrists and ankles into place on the cross. Leaving her there, he went to the display table and picked up a black leather whip with a long, rolled tail and thick braided handle. Returning to center stage, he held up the whip. "This is a dragon tail," he announced. He gripped the tail and ran its length through his fingers. "As you can see, it's thicker and softer than a traditional bullwhip. But it can still pack quite a wallop." He snapped it suddenly, and Zoë flinched as it cracked in the air.

"This particular dragon tail is one of my personal whips, and it's much used, and hence quite soft and pliable. When you first buy a dragon tail, the leather is stiffer, though my tails, which are made from genuine kangaroo leather, are vastly superior to anything else you can find on the market."

He flicked the whip again. "Nevertheless, it's always a good idea to break in any new whip with some practice throws before you use it on your sub." He turned toward Jill. "I assume most of the Doms in this room are already relatively expert in handling single tail whips and floggers, though I'd venture a guess that bullwhips and dragon tails are less popular, primarily because they can do significant damage if not handled properly. But, as with any potentially dangerous tool, if you know what you're doing, the rewards far outweigh the risks."

He faced the audience head on, his gaze falling on Zoë, as he added, "There is nothing more exquisite than the impassioned cry of erotic suffering, and the sublime control of another's sensual reactions." His intensely blue eyes bored into hers, and though she wanted to, Zoë found she couldn't look away. Heat rose in her face as he held her captive with his gaze. Dylan's arm came around her shoulders and he pulled her closer.

Mercifully, Master Cameron shifted his gaze and snapped the whip once more. He turned his attention back to Jill as Zoë let out a breath she hadn't realized she was holding. "We've secured this slave girl on the cross, but if you don't have one of these handy items at home, you can simply have your sub place their hands against the wall and hold their position." Again his gaze fell on Zoë. "It adds a nice bit of psychological bondage—if they move, they get punished."

He began the demonstration, discussing the proper stance, posture, distance, elbow, thumb and wrist action, what parts of the subject's body to target and what to avoid. His Australian accent was charming, despite his inflated ego.

"Take your time," he said, gripping and releasing the whip so the tip snapped across Jill's bottom, making her flinch. "You'll want a slow buildup to get the proper energy flowing." He struck Jill again, still using just the tip of the tail. "Make the throw concise"—the whip struck between Jill's shoulder blades—"determined"—it landed across the backs of her thighs—"and fluid."

He whipped her steadily, the leather snapping and flicking across her bare body. At first Jill was relatively still, but, as her skin reddened, a few welts rising on her ass and thighs, she began to dance on her feet, and arch inward, as if by doing so she could avoid the relentless lash.

"Yes," Master Cameron intoned. "Now you move closer. This creates an S snap, which is much more painful, and hence, more satisfying." The leather throw arced across Jill's upper back several times in rapid succession and, for the first time, her cry was audible and filled with anguish.

Zoë glanced anxiously at Louis, whose expression remained calm, though his hands were clenched in his lap. She glanced at Dylan, whose eyes were fixed on the scene. "When you turn your wrists like this"—Master Cameron danced back and flicked his wrist, the throw catching just beneath Jill's ass—"the horizontal flow allows an undercut." He snapped again along the tender flesh just below Jill's ass and she howled.

"Is she okay?" Zoë couldn't help but whisper urgently to Jill's husband.

"She's fine," he murmured back. "She's right on the edge. He's really good."

Not convinced, but forcing herself to suspend her own concerns, Zoë turned back to watch. Master Cameron was flicking Jill's ass steadily, the crack of leather snapping against skin the only sound in the room, besides Jill's rasping breath.

Then, all at once, her head fell back so her face was lifted to the ceiling, her blond hair streaming down her back. All the tension seemed to drain away, as if her muscles and bones had melted inside her. She sagged in her cuffs, a long, peaceful sigh audible over the continued flicking strokes of the dragon tail.

Dylan's hand closed over Zoë's, his mouth brushing her ear as he whispered, "She's flying." Zoë watched in awe, a little jealous of Jill's ease and grace, wondering if she herself would ever be able to let go enough to get to that kind of a place with a whole audience of people watching.

Master Cameron continued a slow, steady pace, easing his throw until finally the leather was only kissing Jill's reddened, welted flesh. Hank appeared by the stairs and nodded toward Louis, who was instantly on his feet. The two of them moved quickly onto the stage and released Jill from her cuffs. Master Cameron stood on the edge of the platform, again inclining his head like a king accepting his due, as the crowd erupted in applause and hoots of approval.

Louis took Jill tenderly in his arms and helped her from the stage. She appeared dazed but beatifically happy. Michael took center stage and announced details of the whip sale to take place in the lounge later that evening. Dylan leaned in again to Zoë, his arm going around her shoulder, his hand cupping her partially exposed breast. "What do you think, sub girl? Should we buy a dragon tail? I'd love to take you to that place."

~*~

As they moved along the tables set up with Master Cameron's wares, Dylan surreptitiously watched Zoë's reactions. He had seen that look before—the shining eyes, the parted lips, the quick intake of breath as she touched a particular whip, her mind no doubt veering toward the erotic possibilities, as her skin tingled with anticipation. Zoë was clearly a born sub. It was a wonder to Dylan, who had been in touch with his own dominant impulses and desires since he'd been sexually aware, that she could have spent her entire adult life in strictly vanilla relationships. Maybe, it suddenly occurred to him, that was why she'd never settled down with a guy—even if not consciously aware, she was waiting for a Dom.

Was he that Dom?

Dylan picked up one of Master Cameron's ridiculously overpriced but admittedly very fine quality dragon tails. The throw, while a little stiff, was soft enough for immediate use, and the handle was perfectly weighted in his hand. A few sessions, and it would be ready for some serious action.

Zoë was standing in front of a grouping of rattan canes,

staring at them as if they were live and venomous snakes. Master Cameron stood on the other side of the display table, watching her with hooded eyes. Dylan came up behind her and wrapped the long, deceptively soft strip of leather around her torso from behind, pulling her back against him.

"Oh!" she cried, clearly startled at his touch. She twisted around in his leather embrace and then stepped back. He let the whip fall away and held it up for her inspection.

"I like this one. Do you?"

Zoë nodded, her eyes fixed wide on the dragon tail. "It's beautiful, Sir," she breathed.

"Good choice," Master Cameron said with a smile. "Though I think your lady favors the canes."

"No," Zoë blurted, pressing closer to Dylan. "No, I don't."

Master Cameron offered a shrug and then turned away, distracted by a guy asking questions about bullwhips.

It would be a while before Zoë was ready for the delightful intensity of a cane, but Dylan was confident she would get there. For now, he said, "We'll go with the dragon tail. We could test it out tonight. Would you like that?"

He watched the play of emotions on her face—the fear, the desire, the resolution, the determination. Up went her pretty little chin. "Yes, Sir."

"That's my girl." Dylan put his arm around her, pulling her close.

He purchased the whip and they moved together from the

lounge to the main dungeon. There was a large crowd clustered around the spider web in the corner—a restraining device comprised of thick elastic bands woven onto an aluminum frame, excellent for securing a sub in various positions for erotic play.

As they approached, Dylan saw a guy he didn't recognize standing at the center beside a young sub named Lisa. She was naked and bound in the web, her arms and legs spread eagle, her body crisscrossed with welts from two single tails the Dom was wielding, one in each hand. The display was showy, like a Hibachi chef at a touristy Japanese restaurant, but the crowd was eating it up.

Jill and Louis were standing at the edge of the crowd, and Dylan tapped their shoulders. "We're going to the smaller dungeon for a simple scene. We'd love you to be our witnesses," he said quietly.

The two nodded and smiled at Zoë, who smiled back nervously. The four of them moved to the smaller dungeon. There was a scene involving two guys taking place at a far station, their action partially obscured by a folding screen.

New dragon tail in hand, Dylan led his friends to a metal St. Andrew's cross not unlike the one that had been erected on the stage. Dylan considered whether to have Zoë strip or not, and decided this first time out to allow her to keep the corset in place. It was cut such that he had good access to both her upper back and ass. Her thong panties wouldn't interfere.

"Face the cross," he instructed Zoë.

Her eyes flickered from his face to Louis' and then to Jill's.

"May I?" Jill asked Dylan, who nodded.

Jill moved to Zoë. "Courage," she said softly but audibly. "You're in good hands, honey. Master Dylan is the best of the best. This is the beginning of something truly wonderful, I promise." She held out her arms, and Zoë moved into them, her body visibly relaxing. They held each other a moment, and then Jill stepped back, giving Dylan a brief nod.

Zoë faced Dylan, new resolve in her face. "I'm ready, Sir." She faced the cross and lifted her arms, slipping her wrists into the open cuffs toward the top of the cross.

Dylan secured her wrists. "I'm going to leave your feet free," he told her. He stroked her back. He could sense the tension but also the determination. "Remind me," he said, "of your safeword."

"Buyout."

"I'm going to give you twenty strokes," Dylan said. "You will count for us, and thank me when we are done."

"Yes, Sir."

He started easy, as much to acquaint himself with the new whip as to give her a chance to adjust. By the time they reached the count of ten, Zoë was breathing hard and dancing a little on her toes. When he reached fifteen, he let the whip crack with more force. They all watched as a long, white welt rose across both Zoë's ass cheeks and then turned rapidly to an angry red. Zoë cried out, the first real cry of pain, but she managed to push out the word, "Fifteen," a second later.

Dylan gave her a moment to compose herself, and then

struck again, just as hard, this time catching her just beneath the ass with a sharp undercut.

Again she cried out, but again she managed to say the number, though somewhat breathily: "Sixteen!"

Each of the next four strokes was deliberately aimed to leave a parallel welt on her ass. When he was done, Zoë was whimpering steadily, her skin shiny with perspiration, her limbs trembling. He waited, determined to count to three in his head before reminding her of her task, but at the count of two she managed, "Thank you, Sir."

Dylan nodded to Louis, and they stepped forward, each releasing a wrist cuff. As Zoë fell back, Dylan caught her in his arms and spun her toward him, holding her close against his chest. She lifted her face and their lips met, the world around them dissolving away.

Chapter 10

Zoë stroked the soft velvet of her new gown as they zipped along the highway toward The Vault. When Dylan had first selected it from the rack at the BDSM boutique, Zoë had been surprised at his choice of a full-length gown, since he seemed to favor more revealing items like the corset they'd bought the week before. Then she'd tried it on, and the slits up either side were cut nearly to her hips, the bodice, with its built-in bra, barely high enough to cover her nipples.

Though she wasn't used to wearing such revealing clothing, when they were at the club, she found she didn't mind. Though not all the members of The Vault were model-perfect by any means, people seemed comfortable in their own skin. She was surprisingly at ease with the group of people she'd met there, not just because many of them wore even less than she did, but because of the general attitude of non-judgmental acceptance.

Zoë loved both the day-to-day vanilla development of their new relationship, and the sexy, dark and delicious D/s bond that was tested each night in Dylan's private dungeon.

She'd been shy at first at the thought of a public scene, until Dylan had helped her see that The Vault was merely an extension of her training, with the added spark of others witnessing her journey. Tonight Dylan had promised to introduce Zoë to the delights of the hot wax scene station. "You'll especially like when we flog off the cooled wax afterward," he'd joked, and then she'd realized he wasn't joking. The realization both thrilled and frightened her, the thrill outweighing the fear, and sending a jolt of electricity straight to her sex.

The sound of a cell phone ringing through the car's blue tooth system interrupted the smoky jazz playing on the radio. Dylan glanced at the screen and touched something on his steering wheel to connect the call.

"Hey, there, Ed. What's going on? Did you miss the plane?" Dylan's business partner was making the trip down to DC that evening to close an important deal the two of them had been working on for some time.

"I'm not at the airport. It's my dad. He fell down. I'm on my way to the hospital."

"Shit," Dylan swore softly. "Is he okay?"

"Broken hip. He's in a lot of pain. Look, I'm really sorry, Dylan, but you're going to need to step in, if you can. I called the airline. They can switch the reservation to your name, if you're able to go. You know these clients—fucking pains in the ass. After all the hoops you jumped through to restructure the deal to his satisfaction, Harrison has been grousing again about some of the terms. One of us really needs to be there to hold his hand through this last sticky bit. I would hate to see this thing tank at the last minute after all the work we've put in."

Dylan's jaw tightened, his mouth curving down in a frown. Ed continued on the speakerphone, "You've got about an hour to get to the Westchester Airport. I know it's last minute, but can you cover for me?"

Dylan cast an agonized glance at Zoë, who mouthed, "Of

course you can," to him, as she forced down her own disappointment.

Dylan squared his shoulders, gripping the steering wheel tight with both hands. "Yeah, okay. I'm only about twenty minutes from there right now. I'm driving, so text me the details."

Ed blew out an audible sigh of relief. "Okay, great. Let me know how it goes."

"I will. You just focus on taking care of your dad. Talk to you soon."

He ended the connection and turned to Zoë, his face a mirror of her disappointment. "I'm so sorry, Zoë. I was really looking forward to tonight. I know you were too."

Zoë shook her head. "No, don't be silly. I mean, yeah, I was looking forward to it, but there will be plenty of other nights, right?"

"Of course there will." Dylan smiled, and then sighed. "Ed's right—we've spent months putting this deal together and it's been one giant pain in the ass from start to finish, but it's going to make us a whole lot of money once it goes through. It would be a shame if it cratered at the last minute." He shook his head. "Poor Ed. Since his mom died last year, his dad has been a mess. Ed's their only child so..."

Zoë put her hand on Dylan's thigh and gave him a reassuring squeeze. "Hey, you've got to do this. I get it. Really. You can just drop me at your place, grab an overnight bag and—"

"Wait," Dylan interrupted. "We're only a few minutes from the club. Why don't I drop you off there instead? Just because I can't go, doesn't mean you can't. I'm sure Louis and Jill could give you a ride home. I'll give them a call, okay? If it's a problem, we'll both just head home." He looked toward her, his face filled with hope and relief that he'd found a solution.

Though she didn't really like the idea of going to the club without him, she could see it would make him happy to think he hadn't ruined her evening, and so she said brightly, "Sure, that would be perfect." She shrugged and grinned. "Maybe some hot guy will want to scene with me."

"Ha ha." Dylan grinned back, but then, sobering, he added, "Actually, if that seems appropriate and something you'd like to do, I'm totally cool with that."

Zoë started to protest that she had been kidding and no way would she want to do a scene without him there, but Dylan spoke over her. "No, hear me out, Zoë. I actually think it might be an excellent test of your submissive grace. That's the great thing about The Vault. You can trust the folks there. If you're comfortable with an offer, I think you should accept. And I will expect a full accounting of what transpired, and your reactions. Deal?"

Zoë said nothing for several beats as she considered what he said. *If you're comfortable*. Okay, then. The odds were high she would not be comfortable, and so this really was just an academic argument. "Deal," she said. "Call me when you get to DC?"

"It's a promise."

Zoë felt a twinge of anxiety as The Vault's front door was opened to admit her without Dylan's supportive presence. He'd called ahead, however, and she was led directly through the dining room to the table where Jill and Louis already sat, sipping wine, a third glass at the ready for her.

Over dinner, Jill told Zoë about the Sub Club, a submissive support group that met a few times a month, either at The Vault or at a breakfast on weekend mornings. It was a loose affiliation of submissives, mostly women but also a few guys, who met to chat about any issues or concerns they were having either in their personal relationships, or with the whole complex and fascinating D/s lifestyle.

"We talk about any and everything," Jill said. "It's a great opportunity to say exactly what's on your mind, without worrying whether you're being a proper sub. It's a safe place."

"It's an excellent resource," Louis added. "Unfortunately, though most Dominants and would-be Masters have their hearts in the right place, there are some clueless guys out there who don't know what the hell they're doing. It can be very difficult for a sub to confront her Dom, and sometimes she doesn't even realize that what's happening has fallen out of the realm of safe, sane and consensual. The Sub Club can be a good sounding board to help someone get more perspective."

"And a good way for acquaintances to become real friends," Jill said, smiling warmly at Zoë.

Real friends.

Zoë used to have those, hadn't she? Back before she let

her job basically consume her life. How long had it been since she'd just hung out with the girls, shooting the breeze, lamenting or celebrating their latest relationships, and sharing their dreams and hopes? Since Dylan had taken her home two weeks before, it was as if whole layers of a life she thought was all that mattered had been stripped away, returning her to a simpler and more genuine place—a place where love and friendship mattered more than the constant pursuit of money and control. She was ready for friends—real friends.

"Sounds great," Zoë said. "Count me in."

After dinner, Louis excused himself to talk to Michael and Hank about some ideas he had for an upcoming event, and Jill took Zoë over to the long bar that flanked one wall of the old dining room.

"Zoë, meet Betty and Angela," Jill said, introducing Zoë to two women who sat side-by-side on stools at the bar. "They're both members of the Sub Club." Betty was a fifty-something brunette with a round face and a kind smile. She reminded Zoë of her favorite librarian from elementary school, except that she was bare-breasted, heavy silver hoops dangling from her pierced nipples, her back marked with fading and new evidence of a recent whipping. Angela was in her twenties, tall and willowy, with hair dyed silver, the tips a dark blue. She had very pale skin, accentuated by lips painted a deep red. She wore a sheer black silk blouse tucked into a tight black leather mini skirt, her long, shapely legs bare, her feet tucked into Barbie doll stiletto heels.

They exchanged small talk for a few minutes, and then Jill said to Zoë, "Let's go into the dungeon. Louis has given me permission to do a scene, if the mood strikes me. How about you—did Dylan say you can scene without him?"

Zoë nodded. "He did, actually. Though I doubt I will."

"Why not? It can be a great way to test your submissive mettle, if you will. To see how you handle a scene without your lover smoothing the way for you."

"That's kind of what Dylan said. But I don't know," Zoë mused as they walked together into the main dungeon. "It sort of seems like cheating."

Jill shook her head. "Not at all. In fact, that's one of the great things about the scene—you can engage in a truly extraordinary experience with someone without even touching them. A real Dom—he can be incredible in a scene, even if you want nothing to do with him afterward." She laughed, adding, "In those instances, it's about the D/s connection, not sex. It's not the *guy*, it's what he's giving you, and what you give in return. A pure and meaningful exchange of power."

Zoë couldn't help but laugh. "You make it sound like a religious experience."

"Oh, no," Jill countered with a laugh of her own. "It's way better than that. No guilt and shame, just pure, sublime, erotic pleasure. Oh!" she said suddenly, turning her head. "That's Master Kyle over there. He promised me a needle session. He looks like he's alone. I'd better get over there before another sub girl grabs him up!"

"Needles, ugh," Zoë murmured with a shudder, though she followed Jill, who made a beeline for a station where a tall, thin man with dark, brooding eyes was busy setting out rows of plastic-wrapped needles on a black tray.

Jill introduced Master Kyle to Zoë and began to negotiate the terms of a scene with him. "You're free to watch," Master Kyle informed Zoë, looking down his long nose at her, "though I require any sub at my station to kneel quietly on the perimeter, arms behind your back."

Zoë was spared the necessity of refusing by a tap on her shoulder. She turned to see the man she recognized as Master Cameron as he flashed his dazzling smile at her. "Good evening," he said in his charming Australian accent. "You're Jill's friend, aren't you?" He nodded toward Jill, who nodded back with a bright smile, though she was in the process of being bound, facing outward, to an X cross by Master Kyle.

"I thought you were returning to Australia, Master Cameron," Jill said as Master Kyle cuffed her ankles into position. "If I'd known *you* were here tonight…" She trailed off as Master Kyle scowled, and Zoë suppressed a smile.

"Yeah," Master Cameron said. "I'll be staying until the end of the week. So much to see, so much to do," he added, his eyes shifting from Jill to Zoë. "You're here alone?" He looked past her and then back at her face.

"Unfortunately my Dom, Dylan, couldn't be here tonight," Zoë said, missing him acutely at that moment.

"Oh, what a shame," Master Cameron said, though his eyes said otherwise. "Would you care to engage in a scene? Is that permissible?"

Dylan's words drifted into her mind. *An excellent test of your submissive grace.* Recalling the scene on stage with Jill, clearly Master Cameron knew what he was doing. Plus, she didn't want to watch Jill get stuck with a bunch of needles, and what else would she do—wander around the dungeon watching various scenes like a kid with her face pressed up against the window of a toy store?

"It is permissible. I'm not sure, uh…" she stammered, her usual confidence in her ability to handle herself derailed by the newness of the situation. *Just treat it like a business transaction,* she told herself. *This guy is a pro. Negotiate the terms like any other deal, and never let the other guy see you sweat.* Speaking with more confidence, she said, "What did you have in mind?"

"I was thinking we could break in one of my new floggers. Or perhaps one of my other new toys." He indicated the large gear bag slung over his shoulder. "I'm sure we can find something that suits in here." He glanced around the dungeon. "It looks like all the stations are occupied. Perhaps we'll check out the smaller dungeon?"

"Yes, all right," Zoë agreed, relieved at the prospect of a more private scene. She glanced again at Jill. Her blouse was unbuttoned, revealing her bare breasts and narrow torso. She was focused on Master Kyle, who was unwrapping and arranging the needles. He lifted one for Jill's inspection, and Zoë turned away.

Surprisingly, the small dungeon was empty. "All to the good," Master Cameron said. "I prefer a private scene the first time out with a new sub." He pushed the door closed and held out a hand to indicate Zoë should precede him into the room. "Let's sit down a minute and talk about expectations, shall we?"

Zoë noticed a sofa set against the back wall, the only available place in the room to sit, and she moved toward it, wishing he'd left the door open, but not sure enough of herself to say anything. She sat on the sofa. Master Cameron dropped his large gear bag at his feet and sat beside her. He shifted a little so he was facing her. "What's your experience with sensory deprivation?"

"I'm sorry?"

"Being blindfolded, ears stopped, gagged—that sort of thing. You know, hear no evil, see no evil, speak no evil?" He grinned, looking suddenly boyish, and Zoë found herself relaxing.

"I'm pretty new to the scene," she explained. Would he run for the hills if he knew just how new? "But Dylan has introduced to me to bondage and blindfolds. We haven't used a gag or ear plugs, though. I'm not sure I'm comfortable with that."

Master Cameron nodded. "No problem. We'll start slow so I can get a measure of your limits."

That sounded reasonable to Zoë. "Okay."

Master Cameron reached for the gear bag. He unzipped it, revealing a cache of whips, floggers and canes. He lifted out a heavy flogger that was dyed a royal blue. Zoë could smell the rich scent of fine leather.

Though she was excited, she was also nervous, alone with a strange man. She wished Dylan were there now, observing and guiding the process. She was out of her ken, but at the same time she wanted to prove, both to herself and to Dylan, that she was up to the challenge.

As if just thinking about him had somehow conjured his

spirit, she heard his deep, sexy voice of encouragement in her head. *You can do this, Zoë. Make me proud. Show your submissive grace.*

Master Cameron stood and gestured for Zoë to do the same. "Let's start with a flogging, shall we?" He ran his fingers through the suede tresses, pulling them straight. "You'll need to take off that gown," he added, his tone matter-of-fact. "I wouldn't want to ruin it."

Zoë swallowed, her face heating. She knew she was being ridiculous. It wasn't a sexual thing, she reminded herself. No big deal. And she would keep on her panties.

She allowed Master Cameron to unzip the long zipper at the back of her gown. She stepped carefully out of it. Master Cameron took the gown from her and placed it on the sofa.

He didn't ogle her bare breasts, and indeed, barely seemed to notice she was nearly naked, save for thong panties, thigh-high stockings and heels. His matter-of-fact manner reassured her. This guy was a pro, and she could trust him.

"We'll start with your hands behind your head, feet shoulder-width apart," he said. "We'll add restraints as I gauge your comfort level."

That sounded good to Zoë, and she assumed the position, her skin tingling in anticipation of the stinging kiss of leather. He started slowly, just as Dylan did, letting her skin warm and accustom itself to the stroke, and then gradually intensifying as he applied more force to his swing. She closed her eyes, focusing on the sensation, visualizing Dylan standing before her, watching her.

Just when the strokes were edging from sensual pleasure to erotic pain, the flogging stopped. Zoë opened her eyes and twisted back to regard Master Cameron. Had she done something wrong?

"Good," he said with apparent approval. "You handled that well. I'd like to secure your wrists, to give you more balance as we progress."

Zoë, a little wobbly on the high heels, nodded her agreement. She glanced toward the X cross. Master Cameron, following her gaze, shook his head. "I want to suspend you right here." He pointed to the chains hanging from the ceiling just over her head. Zoë swallowed at this pronouncement, but could see no real reason to protest.

He produced a pair of black leather wrist cuffs and some clips from his gear bag. The cuffs were lined with sheepskin, and they felt comforting as he closed them around her wrists and secured the clips to the chains.

He went to the wall and turned a handle attached to a pulley apparatus that caused the chains at her wrists to rise, pulling her arms taut over her head. A tremor of nervous anticipation shuddered its way through her frame, and she glanced at the closed door. "Don't you think we should open that?" she queried.

Master Cameron, who was rummaging in his gear bag again, shook his head. "No. Let's enjoy our privacy while we can." He slipped some things into his pockets and returned to her holding up a satin sash. "I find it helps a sub to relax and focus on the sensations more effectively when visual stimulation is removed."

"I'm not sure," Zoë began, but he cut her off.

"That's okay. I am."

Just go with it, she told herself, trying to ignore the sudden, jagged edge of worry that cut its way into her psyche. Then something occurred to her, and she blurted, "My safeword. You didn't ask for my safeword."

"Right. Apologies." Master Cameron was now standing behind her. He placed the satin blindfold over her eyes and brought the two ends of the sash behind her head. "What's your safeword?"

"Buyout."

"Pardon?"

"Buy. Out," she said slowly and distinctively.

"Buyout," he repeated. "Okay, got it."

She could hear him moving behind her, and then she sensed him standing in front of her. She startled when something cool and hard was pressed between her breasts. "Oh, what is that?"

"It's a cane," Master Cameron said. "A lovely, whippy cane."

The sudden, whooshing sound of something being whipped in the air made Zoë flinch. "I don't like canes," she said quickly. "No canes."

"Oh, I think the lady doth protest too much. I saw the way you were staring at my cane display last week. You crave the purifying experience only a cane can offer. Don't bother to deny it." His voice was playful.

"No, no," Zoë blurted, a tendril of panic curling its way through her gut. "You're wrong. I don't want that. I don't like canes."

The playful tone edged into something harder. "I don't remember asking you if you liked canes. It's not your decision, sub girl. It's mine."

"No, wait," Zoë insisted, confused and upset. "That's not right. We're supposed to negotiate a scene—"

Her words were cut off by something firm pressed over her mouth. It took her a second to realize it was his hand. She twisted her head, instinctively trying to step away, but her cuffed wrists prevented her. "Stop all that nonsense," Master Cameron said with a small, unpleasant laugh. "Just go with it, love. You know you want it."

He removed his hand. Shaken and shocked, Zoë blurted, "Buyout! Buyout, buyout, buyout!" Panting, she waited for him to remove the blindfold and let her down.

Nothing happened.

An ice pick of real fear stabbed through Zoë's innards. "I said my safeword!" she cried. "Let me down this instant. I've changed my mind."

Her shock deepened when Master Cameron just laughed, the sound harsh and derisive in her ears. "Don't be ridiculous. You're way overreacting here, silly girl. We haven't even started yet. You can't end a scene before it starts. Don't you know that?" He patted the top of her head. "It'll be fabulous, I promise."

Zoë opened her mouth to shout her protest, but the sound was cut off by a hard hand pressed hard over her lips. "Stop all the fuss. Behave yourself, sub girl. You're being ridiculous."

His hand was removed, and this time Zoë screamed, but almost immediately something hard and foul tasting was shoved between her teeth, cutting off her cry. She tried to expel the rubbery ball pressing her tongue back toward her throat, but found she couldn't. Master Cameron was behind her, buckling the thing onto the back of her head.

Zoë's heart was beating so hard she could feel it knocking against her chest. She felt dizzy with fear and if she hadn't been held up by the cuffs, she would have fallen. She tried to scream again but only managed to gurgle. Surely if he understood her terror was genuine, he would let her down. He would stop this crazy, terrifying game.

Safe, sane and consensual. Weren't those the bywords everyone in the scene lived by? What was happening? How could this asshole not be getting it? She had to try again. "Get this thing off me! Let me down! Buyout, buyout, buyout!" she cried behind the gag, but all that came out was, "Mmmph mmph grggl mmph!"

"Shh, you don't need to play these games with me. I get it—you're the damsel in distress, but I don't really go for role-play. Anyway, I can see right through you. Just go with it, love. You know what they say"—again the unpleasant laugh—"if you can't fight it, you might as well lie back and enjoy it."

Outraged, Zoë jerked in her chains, but to no avail. She jumped when she felt the light, stinging tap of what must be the cane against her ass. It flew rapidly over her skin and she could hear its clicking, pattering sound moving in syncopated rhythm against the pounding of her heart.

As new as she was to the scene, Zoë knew what was happening was wrong. She also understood there wasn't a damn thing she could do about it.

Okay, okay. Just get through this. You can do this. You can deal. He isn't really hurting you. It's some kind of fucked up mind game, but you can handle it. Breathe. Relax. Flow with it. Harness and use the fear, like Dylan taught you.

"That's better," Master Cameron said soothingly. "I can feel you relaxing. I told you it would be fine if you just go with it. Much better. I think I'll just lock that door to assure our privacy, hmm?"

Zoë shook her head violently, to no avail. She heard the sound of a lock being turned, and then the clomp of his boots as he returned to her. There was a sudden, whooshing sound and then a searing shock of pain sliced its way through her senses.

"Fuck!" she screamed against the gag, though it came out more as a phlegmy *ugglh*. "Buyout! Buyout!" she gargled again, though she no longer held out any hope he would pay attention, or care.

Another slice of pain cut its away across her ass, followed by yet another on the backs of her thighs. She twisted and jerked in her effort to get away from the cane, and as she moved one of her shoes fell off, leaving her off-balance and forced to stand on tiptoe with one foot.

Suddenly Zoë remembered the universal safeword sign Dylan had taught her, and she began to clench and unclench her fists furiously above the cuffs, while still struggling to form her safeword with her tongue pressed far back in her mouth.

"Give in to it, love," Master Cameron crooned behind her. "You'll never fly if you don't spread your wings."

The cane continued to whoosh and strike, each cut leaving a fiery line of pain on Zoë's flesh. Again and again she continued to clench and unclench her fists. Tears were wetting the satin blindfold, and her nose was running, the snot mingling with the drool dripping down her chin. Fear, pain and rage bloomed like an atomic mushroom in her gut, and still the cane came down again, and again, and again.

Finally Zoë sagged in her cuffs, trying to swallow the saliva pooling in her mouth, praying the nightmare would end soon.

"That's it," the monster behind her urged. "You're nearly there. I can feel it."

Suddenly Zoë's ears pricked to a sound from across the room. She processed it through her muddled brain, and realized it was the doorknob jiggling. "Mmph!" she cried out desperately.

"Shit," Master Cameron muttered behind her.

"Open the door," a deep, masculine voice called from the other side of the door. "Now."

There was the sound of a key turning, and then the door

opening. Zoë heard raised voices, Master Cameron's in protest, another man with anger, and then Jill's voice rising in a wail. "Zoë!"

Relief hurtled through Zoë's consciousness and at the same time the tight grip she'd been keeping on her sanity ebbed away. Sudden bursts of white light mushroomed behind her eyelids, and all sound in the room was drowned out by a persistent ringing in her ears. The world tilted on its axis, and Zoë slid down, down and down into a deep, dark and silent place.

Chapter 11

Buyout. Buyout. Buyout!

Zoë's eyes flew open, the word still echoing in her ears. Blue eyes were peering into her face. For several seconds she stared into those eyes with zero recognition. She had no idea where she was or what was happening.

The eyes moved back so Zoë could focus on the face, which broke into a smile of relief. It was Jill Sutton. "Oh, thank god. She's coming out of it. Are you okay, honey? You gave us quite a scare."

Zoë lay on her stomach, her head cradled in her arms. She lifted her head to see Jill sitting beside her. Something touched Zoë's back and she twisted around to see a man holding a tube of something in one hand. He had a stethoscope around his neck, which looked incongruous against his black leather vest. Zoë shifted her gaze back to Jill in confusion. "What? Who?"

"It's okay, honey." Jill patted her soothingly. "Michael is a medical doctor. He's just making sure you're all right."

Zoë wrinkled her forehead as she tried to concentrate through a fog of confusion. Why was she lying on this bed surrounded by these people? How had she come to be here? A feeling of terrible danger clung to her senses like the sticky mesh of a spider's web, and yet Jill was smiling at her, her expression calm and reassuring.

A firm hand pressed at her shoulder, pushing her gently back to the mattress. "Lie still a moment longer, please, Zoë." Michael's voice was deep, his tone kind. "You fainted and were out for several minutes. It might take a few moments to orient yourself. Take it easy. Just rest while I finish treating your back."

"My back? What happened..." Zoë trailed off, memory suddenly returning in a gush, the whole horrible scene with Master Cameron dumping into her mind like a bucket of sewage. "Oh," she whispered. "Oh my god."

Michael continued applying salve to her back, his touch soothing the fiery sting of welts that had come awake along with her return to consciousness. He patted her shoulder. "There, now. There is some bleeding where he broke the skin, but I don't think there will be any scarring. Do you think you can sit up now?"

Zoë nodded. Michael and Jill both reached supportively for her as she struggled into an upright position. Jill draped a silk kimono-type robe over Zoë's shoulders and helped her slip her arms into it. Though the sense of imminent danger had dissipated, as Zoë wrapped the garment around herself, she realized her hands were shaking.

Michael handed her a bottle of water, which she accepted with thanks. The cool water was refreshing, and her mind began to clear as the doctor did a quick check of her vital signs and questioned her as to her physical and mental state of mind.

Finally satisfied, he turned to Jill. "Okay, she's going to be fine after a little decompression and debriefing. I'll leave her in your capable hands." He frowned as he added, "I want to go see what's up with *Master* Cameron. He's got a hell of a lot of explaining to do."

Michael left the room, closing the door softly behind him. Zoë realized there were two more people in the room. Betty was sitting in wingback chair opposite the sofa. She leaned forward. "That was a bad scene that prick put you through," she said darkly.

Angela sat on the carpet beside the daybed, leaning against it. She reached up and touched Zoë's knee, shaking her head in sympathetic agreement.

Zoë realized she was trembling, and she wiped the tears trickling down her cheeks with surprise. "I don't cry," she announced, aware she was telling herself more than these three women who were all staring at her so intently. "I haven't cried since I was five years old."

Jill put her arms around Zoë and murmured softly, "It's okay, baby. Everyone cries."

Something cracked in Zoë's chest at these words, and the floodgates opened. She buried her face helplessly in Jill's warm, strong embrace. "It's okay, baby," Jill crooned again. "It's all okay. Crying is good. Let it out. Let it go." She stroked Zoë's hair. Ugly, noisy sobs wracked her body, yanked from somewhere deep inside. Zoë felt as if sorrow was being dredged from deep in her bones.

Her tears finally spent, she lifted her head, exhausted but oddly peaceful. She took the handful of tissues Jill held out to her and wiped her face, finally turning to the others with an embarrassed smile. "You guys must think I'm such a baby."

"A baby?" Angela said, the indignation clear in her tone.

"Are you kidding? After what happened? The bastard should be shot!"

"Where is he?" Zoë asked. "Where is Ma—" She stopped herself. He didn't deserve the title. "Where is that bastard, Cameron?"

"Hank and Louis are questioning him," Jill said. "He broke all kinds of rules with what went on in there. They don't take that kind of stuff lightly here at The Vault. That guy's in big trouble, and not just with you."

"Dylan," Zoë said suddenly, the need to see him, to be held in his arms nearly overwhelming her. She looked around for her purse. She saw it sitting atop her gown, which was neatly folded on a sideboard that ran the length of one wall. "I need to call Dylan."

"Louis called him right away," Jill said, patting her hand. "He cut his meeting short. He's on his way back now."

"He's heading back to New York? Now?" Zoë absorbed this, relief warring with guilt. She knew how important closing this deal was for him.

As if reading her mind, Jill said, "Don't worry about his business dealings, Zoë. Whatever he was doing, you're more important. Louis would do the same thing in a heartbeat. It's what love is about, honey. Being there for the person you love. There is no higher priority."

"We're new," Zoë said by way of explanation to the other two women. "We haven't really used that word yet—the L word." She almost managed a grin.

"Trust me, honey," Jill said emphatically. "I've known Dylan a long time, and the boy is smitten. The L word, as you call it, might as well be plastered on his forehead and branded on his butt. Subs may be the ones who are 'owned'"—she drew air quotes around the word—"but you already own Dylan's heart. I guarantee it."

Zoë found she was smiling, Jill's words like a salve on the emotional wound caused by Cameron's betrayal. "Meanwhile," Jill continued, "though this isn't the introduction any of us would have wanted, welcome to the Sub Club."

"Welcome," Betty and Angela echoed.

Betty reached for something by her chair, and held up a bottle. "Care for a shot of the good stuff? This is an excellent Cognac I've been saving for a special occasion. Now that Dr. Michael gave his okay, it's time for some *real* medicine." She grinned.

"Absolutely," Zoë said, surprised to find she could laugh. Angela went to the sideboard and returned with four glasses. Betty poured several fingers of brandy into a glass and handed it to Zoë, and then poured some for each of the others.

When they all had a glass, Jill lifted hers in a toast and the others followed suit. "To the newest member of the Sub Club. Welcome, Zoë."

They all drank. The brandy was a fine one, and Zoë savored the first sip on her tongue. It tasted smoky and a little sweet. She sipped again, and the burn felt good as it bloomed in her chest. The small, cozy room, she finally noticed, was softly lit with indirect lighting. Flames flickered on a series of tall, fat candles on a nearby table, the smell of melting wax, lavender and chamomile scenting the air.

She leaned back carefully against the sofa, the welts marking her back and ass still tender and stinging. "Man," she said. "I feel like I've been run over with a steamroller." She took another sip of the fortifying brandy.

"You were, in a way," Jill said, her tone serious. "Your trust was violated. That's a real kick in the gut, no matter how you look at it. If you feel up to it, tell us what happened, honey."

Before answering, Zoë asked, "How did you know to come find me?"

"Master Kyle and I were done with my scene, and I was wondering where you were, so I went looking. When I found the door to the small dungeon was locked, I knocked, but there was no answer. Something didn't feel right to me, so I went and got Michael. He was in the office and we looked at the security monitor and saw what was happening. It was clear you were making the universal safeword hand signal, and equally clear he wasn't paying attention."

"You never saw anybody run so fast," Angela interjected. "The two of them took off like they were shot out of a cannon."

"Security monitor?" Zoë asked, not following.

"Yeah," Betty added, "Michael and Hank keep security cameras in every scene room as a safety precaution. Occasionally scenes go a little haywire, though I'm not aware of anything like this ever having happened before."

"Me neither," Jill agreed. "You would think Master

Cameron would know better, surely." She shook her head, consternation on her face. "I just don't get it. I had such a great scene with him on stage. How could things have gone so wrong?"

"No witnesses," Angela suggested darkly. "At least, he didn't realize there were any. He must have figured he could do whatever the fuck he wanted. Some so-called Masters are really just bullies in Doms' clothing."

"Was he just clueless," Betty asked Zoë, "or was there actual bad intent?"

Zoë thought about it before answering, going over the bizarre, frightening events in her head. "At first I thought he just wasn't getting it, and maybe I was to blame because I'm new to the scene, and wasn't entirely sure what I was doing. But then I said my safeword. I said it over and over, and he didn't give a shit. He laughed at me." She shuddered as the horrible memories came tumbling back in all-too-vivid detail, tears springing again to her eyes.

Jill put her arm comfortingly around Zoë. "You don't have to talk about it yet, honey, if you aren't ready."

Zoë shook her head resolutely and angrily blinked away the tears. "No. It's okay. Fuck him. He's not going to hijack my wonderful experience with BDSM. No way am I going to let the son of a bitch do that to me."

"You go, girl!" Angela cried enthusiastically, and the other two women laughed and clapped their approval.

Zoë smiled wanly. Then she steeled herself, and told them exactly what had happened. The women's faces darkened as she spoke, each of them hanging on every word. Instead of feeling weakened by the telling, Zoë felt empowered. It was good to be *heard*.

When she was done, Angela picked up a pretty brass bowl from the end table beside her chair and handed it to Jill, who in turn handed it to Zoë. The bowl was etched with symbols and designs, a small wooden dowel resting inside it.

She looked up at the women. "What's this?"

"It's a Tibetan singing bowl," Jill explained. "Run the dowel around the rim of the bowl. It makes a pretty sound."

Zoë picked up the dowel, not entirely sure what she was doing. She rubbed the side of the dowel along the perimeter of the bowl and a small, bell-like sound emanated from it. "Oh," she said softly as the sound grew stronger. "Am I doing that?"

"You are," Jill confirmed.

"The bowls are used for meditation, deep relaxation and holistic healing," Betty explained. "We use it in the Sub Club as a kind of repository for negative shit."

"Yeah," Angela continued, leaning forward, "now that you've shared the bad scene in a safe place, you can let go of it. Just put it right in the bowl and let the music wipe it away." She mimed dropping something into the bowl and then rubbed her hands together for emphasis. "Done. Gone."

Zoë continued stroking the rim of the bowl with the dowel. She quite liked the concept of a "repository for negative shit." Closing her eyes, she envisioned dropping the whole nasty, terrifying scene, and *Master* Cameron along with it, into the bowl, and then letting the contents blow away on the air of its pure, sweet sound.

Finally she dropped the dowel softly into the bowl, letting the last of the music die away. She looked up at the women, all of whom were watching her with kind, attentive smiles. She felt light, the terrible weight of what had happened somehow lifted from her psyche.

"Thank you," she said simply to her new friends.

"You're welcome," they replied in unison.

Then they all laughed, Zoë along with them.

~*~

Dylan raised his hand to pound on The Vault's main door and was startled when it opened before his fist could come into contact with the wood. Louis and Michael stood just inside. "Where is she?" Dylan demanded, stumbling inside. "And where's that bastard son of a bitch asshole whip maker?"

He realized he was clenching his left hand into a fist at his side, his right hand clutching his briefcase. He was still dressed in his suit slacks and dress shirt, his tie loosened at his throat, his jacket slung over his arm. Fortunately, the meeting had gone smoothly, and was nearly at its conclusion when the call had come through from Louis. Normally he wouldn't have taken a personal call during a business meeting, but he knew Louis wouldn't be calling just to chat—not when Dylan had charged him with keeping an eye on Zoë that evening and seeing her safely home.

Excusing himself, he'd taken the call. When he'd returned

to the table, something in his face must have made it clear he wasn't blowing smoke when he informed them he had an emergency at home and had to cut things short. Donald Harrison had surprised him by offering him the use of his private jet and pilot, allowing him to make it to the club in an astonishing hour and a half.

"Calm down," Louis said. "Zoë is in good hands. She's with Jill and the girls."

"I did a thorough exam," Michael added. "She's got a few nasty welts, and of course she's shaken up, but she'll be fine. The last thing she needs right now is for you to go bursting in and upsetting her all over again. Just take a second, okay? Come back to the office so Hank can give you the full story. Then you can go to Zoë, okay, buddy?"

Dylan blew out a breath of frustration, but nodded, recognizing the wisdom of their advice. "Yeah, okay."

They made their way through the club to the back office, where Hank was waiting. Once the door was closed behind them, Dylan looked around, half expecting to see Cameron. He realized he was clenching his fists again, already imagining the satisfying crunch of bone as he smashed that smug, handsome face. "Where is he?" he demanded.

"He's gone," Hank said. "We sent him packing."

"What? I wanted to see him," Dylan said angrily. "He had no right—"

"He's gone as much for your sake as anything," Louis interjected. "The last thing you need right now is to beat up some guy because you're pissed off. That won't solve anything, and you know that, if you stop a minute and cool your jets."

"We read him the riot act," Michael added. "He's not welcome here, and I'll make sure no one else in the BDSM community has anything to do with him. He's blacklisted from this moment forward."

"Yeah," Hank added. "And if he knows what's good for him, he'll get the fuck out of town and never come back."

Dylan sank into one of the chairs in front of the desk, tugging at his tie and pulling it off. Michael went to the small refrigerator in the corner of the room and returned, holding out a bottle of beer in Dylan's direction. Dylan accepted it, twisted off the cap and took a long pull. "Okay. I'm calm, I promise. Tell me what went down, and then I want to see my girl."

Though Dylan had the basics from Louis' phone call, Hank explained in more detail what they'd witnessed on the security monitor. "Cameron claimed it was all consensual, but it was clear from the video stream that she was in distress. And his locking the door…" Hank glowered, shaking his head. "We're going to have that lock removed first thing in the morning. Fortunately, we got to her fast, thanks to Jill."

"Fuck," Dylan swore, his voice cracking. "This is all my fault. I pushed Zoë into this. I essentially ordered her to engage in a scene without me. I should have been there. I should have protected her."

"Stop," Louis said, putting his hand firmly on Dylan's shoulder. "You can't take the blame for someone else being a total asshole. None of us knew Cameron was a fraud. He'd scened with Jill, for god's sake, in front of us all. There was no way to know what happened was going to happen."

"What Zoë needs now from you isn't self-recrimination and certainly not pity," Hank added. "She needs to see your quiet strength and determination to help her deal with what happened. She needs to know you don't blame her one iota for what happened, and that you can move forward as a couple to heal whatever damage was done."

"Yeah. I know you guys are right." Dylan ran his hands over his face. He looked around at his friends and managed a smile. "Thanks for talking me back from the ledge. I need to see Zoë now, okay?"

He stood, struggling to keep the desperation he felt tamped down in front of the others. He had encouraged her to scene without him, and some fucking bastard had violated her trust. God, would she forgive him for what had happened? Would he forgive himself?

Forcing himself to speak calmly, Dylan said, "Take me to her, please."

Louis led Dylan to the recovery room. The door was closed, and Louis rapped softly and then turned the knob. As the door opened, Dylan saw Zoë nestled on the daybed beside Jill, her feet tucked under her, looking very young. Dylan wasn't entirely sure what he'd been expecting, but he was surprised to see all the women were laughing, Zoë included. When he came closer, he could see she had been crying, and a fault line opened in a ragged, painful line across his heart.

In two strides, Dylan was the across the room, his arms outstretched. To his relief and joy, Zoë flew into his arms. She nuzzled her face against his neck as he held her tight. He was vaguely aware of the others leaving, but he couldn't let go of Zoë long enough to pay too much attention.

As the door clicked quietly closed, he moved toward the daybed and settled back against it, Zoë still cradled in his arms. "Baby, baby, oh baby," he whispered. "I'm so sorry."

Zoë pulled back, gently disengaging from his embrace. "I'm okay, Dylan. Jill and the others are amazing."

"I should have been here." Tears momentarily blurred Dylan's vision. He blinked them away.

"You were closing an important deal," Zoë replied, shaking her head. "I feel terrible that you were dragged away like this."

"Are you kidding me? Nothing in this world is more important to me than you." As he said it, he knew in his heart it was absolutely true.

Zoë stroked Dylan's cheek, a soft smile on her face. "Thank you, Sir." Love bloomed inside him like a flower unfurling in time-lapse photography. "The girls really helped me work my way through it. I understand now I should have followed my gut. I let him get me in a compromising position when I wasn't entirely comfortable. I didn't trust myself enough, and as a result, I ended up giving that bastard too much power."

"That asshole betrayed your trust. What he did is tantamount to rape. He violated you. I would totally understand if you want to give this whole thing a break for a while."

Zoë shook her head. "No, no," she said softly but emphatically. "I didn't let him in enough for that. The violation was superficial. He frightened me, yes, but I won't give him that kind of power, Dylan. I remain intact. I promise."

Dylan took Zoë's hand, squeezing it, his heart full, in awe of this amazing woman. "I love you, Zoë." He paused a moment to let those words sink in for them both. Zoë said nothing, though her eyes sparkled as if lit by an inner fire. He repeated more firmly, "I love you so damn much. I am so, so sorry this happened."

"I love you, too, Dylan. And I'm okay. I promise."

They grinned at each other like kids for several moments. Then Zoë said, "Hey, did you ever ride horses when you were a kid?"

Dylan shook his head, confused by the line of questioning, but going along. "Nah. I'm a city boy, born and bred."

"Well, I did. And the first thing you learn is if your horse throws you, you just dust yourself off and get right back on." She shifted so she was facing him. "You talk about the courage it takes to submit, right?" As Dylan nodded, she continued, "It takes courage to dominate, too—don't think I don't get that. You want to give your sub that intensity of experience she craves, but at the same time, you feel a responsibility to keep her safe from harm. You feel right now like you failed in that regard—like you failed me."

Dylan opened his mouth to deny it, but realized it was true. He said nothing.

Zoë shrugged, her chin lifting with the determination he had first witnessed during their business dealings together. "Understand this—you didn't fail me. Or us. Neither of us got as far as we have in our lives by slinking away and licking our wounds when we get thrown. I can't speak for you, Dylan, but I, for one, want to get right back into the saddle. The experience we've shared over these past few weeks together has completely changed and opened my world and my life in a way I never dreamed possible. I'm not about to let that go because of some bully in Dom's clothing."

Dylan laughed in surprise and then shook his head with admiration. "You're a wise woman, Zoë. And you're right. If you're still willing to be a part of this journey with me, I want to be a Dom worthy of claiming your submission."

As if by some silent accord, they both stood. Dylan reached for Zoë, aching to kiss her. But she held him at arms' length as she looked up at him with a clear, somber gaze. "And I," she said softly, "already belong to you, Sir."

Chapter 12

The four of them sat around the table in The Vault's dining room, sipping coffee and port. Louis was regaling them with a funny story about his first fumblings as a Dom back in his college days, when there was no such thing as the Internet. Dylan was only half listening, unable to take his eyes off his lovely sub girl.

Zoë's diamond choker slave collar glittered around her throat. In the two months since Dylan had placed it around her neck, she hadn't removed it. The matching ring he'd had made was nestled in a small box in his pocket, and he fingered it now as he tried to focus on Louis' words.

"So I posted a want ad in the back of this underground BDSM magazine I'd picked up at a sleazy adult bookstore. I got some responses, and I ended up meeting this girl in a bar. She was older than me, with lots of teased blond hair and tons of makeup, but she looked pretty hot, and I was twenty-one and horny as a goat, so I wasn't that particular," Louis said with a grin. "We had a couple of drinks, and the chemistry seemed right, so when she suggested I come back to her place, I said, hell yeah.

"It was the first time I'd ever used a flogger, and she seemed to really be getting off on it, and I was so excited I nearly ejaculated just from the experience. When I was done flogging her, the girl got on her knees and"—he glanced at Jill and then Zoë, censoring himself in advance—"thanked me for the flogging. Then she started to do this strip tease, and that's when I figured out that *she* was actually a *he*."

Dylan had heard the story before. He watched with amusement as Zoë processed what Louis had just said. "Wait, what? She was a *guy*?"

"Yep," Louis confirmed with a bemused shrug. "Turns out the magazine where I'd posted the ad catered to the gay and cross-dressing population in the scene. "

"So what did you do? What did he, I mean, she, do?" Zoë asked.

"I thanked him, uh, her for the experience, zipped up my jeans and beat a hasty retreat. She just laughed, called me a clueless kid, and told me not to get my scrawny ass caught in the door on the way out. It was pretty embarrassing, but I've done worse. There was one time—"

"Louis, dear"—Jill smiled sweetly at her husband—"I know Dylan and Zoë would love to sit all night and listen to your stories, but you promised me a turn at the wax station tonight?" Her voice lifted in a question, but Louis got the hint.

"Yeah, I did, didn't I? How about you two? Going to do a scene tonight?"

Zoë put her hand on Dylan's arm, her fingers cool against his skin. They'd returned to The Vault a number of times in the months since that asshole Cameron had pulled his stunt, and though Zoë remained receptive and fearless in their deepening exploration of BDSM, she hadn't wanted to engage in another public scene, and Dylan hadn't pressed her, nor would he now. When the time was right, she would know it, and if that time never came, he had assured her that was fine with him, and he meant it.

He started to tell Louis no, but something in the press of Zoë's fingers on his arm kept him silent. She glanced from him to Jill, and Dylan followed her gaze. A silent conversation seemed to take place between the two women. Jill gave Zoë a small, encouraging nod.

Zoë lifted her chin and said, "Yes, I think we will do a scene tonight, Louis." She turned to Dylan, her eyes sparkling. "I'm ready, Sir," she whispered. "I want others to witness our continuing journey."

Pride in her courage and grace swelled inside him, and Dylan replied, "I want that, too, sub girl." He turned to Louis and Jill. "After your wax play, would you be our witnesses?"

"We can play with wax any old time," Jill said with an emphatic shake of her head. "I can't think of anything I'd rather do or anywhere I'd rather be right now than watching the two of you do a scene together."

"Agreed," Louis said.

~*~

The four of them moved through the crowded dungeon looking for an empty station. It was a Saturday night and a full moon to boot, and every member of the club seemed to have come out to celebrate their kink with friends.

Zoë's heart fluttered and swooped like a hummingbird. She clutched gratefully at Dylan's hand as they edged past naked and leather-clad people with whips, floggers, rope and chain.

The air was laced with the scent of sweat and arousal, moans of ecstasy and cries of pain weaving in harmony around them.

"I don't see an open station," Dylan said at last, as they continued to move through the crowd.

"We could go to the small dungeon," Zoë said, though just the words made her mouth go suddenly dry. She'd meant what she said about getting back in the saddle in their BDSM exploration, but memories and nightmares of the horrific scene with Cameron had continued to plague her, especially in the first few weeks afterward. She'd steered clear of the small dungeon, afraid it might trigger the bad memories, but she told herself now she was done with that. It was giving Cameron too much power—allowing him to take up space in her head that he didn't deserve.

Dylan glanced down at her, the concern in his eyes making it clear he understood her fears. "Are you sure, sweetheart?"

Ironically, this acknowledgment of her fears somehow gave Zoë the courage and certainty she needed, and she replied stoutly, "Absolutely sure. It's just a room, Dylan. There are no ghosts there, unless we give them access."

He smiled and placed a comforting hand on the small of her back as they made their way to the small dungeon, Louis and Jill behind them. There was already another scene in progress in the room. Mark, a submissive male owned by Mistress Laura, was suspended by his wrists from the chains Cameron had used to secure Zoë. He was naked, and another man was kneeling in front of him, arms bound with rope behind his back, Mark's cock thrust down his throat. Mistress Laura stood behind Mark, cracking a wicked single tail against his flesh.

Dylan led Zoë to the X cross. He dropped his gear bag to the ground and said, "I'm thinking a full body flogging—"

"No."

Dylan stopped mid-sentence and stared at her.

Zoë hadn't meant to blurt it out like that, and she quickly amended, "What I mean, Sir, is please, will you use the cane?"

The surprise was evident on Dylan's face. Since the debacle with Cameron, he'd made it clear that while he would one day like to incorporate the cane into their erotic play, he would wait until she asked for it. She wasn't entirely certain what made her so sure she was ready tonight, but in her bones she knew she was.

Concern was etched into her Dom's features. "I don't think—" he began.

"Dylan." Louis cut him off, placing a hand on his shoulder. "If I may intervene, I suggest you honor her request."

"Yes." Jill, who had recently been encouraging Zoë in their weekly Sub Club meetings to take the step back into public scening, added, "Trust your sub's instincts, Sir, even if you don't entirely trust your own."

Dylan nodded slowly. A change moved over his face, his mouth lifting in a sensual curve that edged into something exciting, even dangerous. "Who do you belong to, Zoe?"

Zoe stared into the dark fire that had ignited in his eyes and felt heat move through her body like the kiss of a flame, melting her core. "You, Sir," she whispered, not trying to hide the reverence in her tone.

Dylan cupped her breasts beneath the leather of her corset, and then slipped his fingers into the bodice. He lifted her breasts so they popped out of their leather casing. Zoë kept her eyes fixed on her Master as he rolled her nipples between his fingers. She couldn't suppress the small moan as they hardened to points beneath his touch.

Letting her go, Dylan bent down and unzipped his gear bag. He lifted out a long, whippy cane, the handle wrapped in dark blue suede. They'd chosen the cane together, but this would be its first use.

He held it up for Zoë to see. Her engorged nipples throbbed even while her gut tightened with nervous anticipation. "Take off your skirt," he ordered quietly.

Zoë untied the sash of her long velvet skirt and stepped carefully out of it. The corset came only to her hips, its garters holding up sheer black stockings. She wore no panties.

"Face the cross, sub girl," Dylan instructed, the quiet power in his voice sending a shivery thrill through Zoë's body. "I will give you what you crave."

She leaned her midriff against the intersection of the smooth wood and lifted her arms, placing her wrists into the open leather cuffs. Dylan clipped the cuffs closed and then crouched behind her to secure her ankles. She leaned into the cross, secure and snug in her bonds. Her entire body thrummed with anticipation.

In spite of her desire, the first stinging taps of the cane

against her ass made Zoë flinch. Without meaning to, she clutched her hands into fists over her cuffs, and had to fight the sudden, unwelcome rush of panic threatening to wash over her. Cameron's words slithered into her brain: *I don't remember asking you if you liked canes. It's not your decision, sub girl. It's mine.*

"Zoë, find your grace." Dylan's voice pulled her back to the present. "Relax your hands. Breathe deeply and remember where it is you want to go. I will take you there."

Zoë uncurled her fingers, drew in a deep breath and let it out slowly. She wasn't alone at the mercy of an abusive bully. She was here with her Master, who would keep her safe and cherish her always, and surrounded by friends who served as witnesses to the grace Dylan was helping her to nurture and explore.

Grounded once more, Zoë said calmly, "Thank you, Sir. I'm ready to continue."

"Good girl. You please me." The cane resumed its warming tap, stirring the blood flow beneath her skin and giving her time to acclimate to its stinging kiss. The cane was different than the engulfing, thuddy embrace of the flogger—its touch sharper and more defined—but the same dark flame whooshed to life deep in Zoë's belly as the cane began its scourging dance in earnest.

Safe in the arms of the man she loved above all else, Zoë was able to let go of the last lingering remnants of fear. Dylan would keep her safe. Sir would give her the gift of erotic pain and pleasure she craved. As he always did, he would weave them together into pure, golden, heavenly sensation.

Strokes of fire ignited over her sweat-slicked skin. Instead of resisting them, she arched back into the heat. It hurt, oh fuck, it hurt! But that was okay. No, it was better than okay—it was essential. "More," Zoë panted wantonly. "More, more, more!"

The cane whipped through the air, followed a fraction of a second later by the thwacking sound of rattan on flesh, and then the ragged, gasp of Zoë's cries. Again and again the pattern was repeated, until the sounds blended together in discordant harmony.

And then slowly, sweetly, inexorably, the cacophony eased itself into a cool, rushing wind blowing Zoë's hair back from her face and kissing away any trace of pain. Giving of herself completely, Zoë took to the heavens and soared…

~*~

Dylan watched the transformation with awe. He glanced back at Louis and Jill, who were watching them, eyes shining. Several other people had wandered into the small dungeon during the caning. The three who had been there when they'd entered had finished their scene and they, too, were watching, transfixed. The room was utterly silent, save for the swish of the cane and Zoë's slow, deep breathing.

Dylan eased the intensity of the caning until he was only stroking her skin with the lightest kiss of rattan. Her head had fallen back. Her eyes were closed, lips softly parted, serenity and acceptance lighting her features as if a small flame burned from within.

Louis took the cane from Dylan's hands as Dylan moved closer to Zoë. He ran his fingers lightly over her back and ass.

Zoë's flesh was beautifully marked with long, dark pink welts that would probably remain for a few hours before they faded away.

Crouching, he released her ankles and then stood, leaning gently into her as he released the wrist cuffs. Zoë fell heavily against him. She sighed the soft, deep sigh of someone whose feet had still not quite returned to earth. Dylan held her for several long moments, his heart aching with love and pride, his cock hard as steel.

He heard the soft click of the door behind him. Glancing back, he saw with surprise that the room was empty. A yellow cloth hanging from a corner of the room caught his eye. Dylan chuckled. Good old Louis.

~*~

Zoë gently disengaged from her lover's arms. He let her go as she turned to face him. "What happened?" she asked, looking around the empty room. "Where did everyone go?"

"We're being offered privacy." Dylan pointed toward the corner, where a towel hung over the security camera. "It's a courtesy long-standing Vault members extend to one another from time to time. No one is watching. No one will come in until we open that door."

He took her in his arms and kissed her for a long time. When he finally let her go, he asked, "Do you trust me, sub girl?"

"With my life, Sir."

"Show me. Turn around so your back is to me. Fall back

into my arms."

The Trust game—that first day in Dylan's dungeon came back to Zoë. It was hard to believe how far she had come—how far they had come—in their D/s journey. Without hesitation, she did as he asked, certain beyond a doubt he would be there to catch her.

Strong arms encircled her as she fell back, and Dylan brought her around so she was facing him. "You please me, sub girl," he said with a smile, though his eyes were hooded with lust. Dominant sensuality radiated from him like an aura.

Zoë's body answered in kind, her nipples hardening to pebbles, her cunt moistening and swelling like unfurling flower petals. She fingered the row of perfect diamonds that studded her slave collar as she stared up at her Master.

The caning had been perfect—exceeding anything she could have imagined, and leaving her exhilarated and pulsing with desire. A shimmer of heat moved its way over her skin as Dylan regarded her with glittering eyes.

"Fuck me," she whispered hoarsely, beyond caring if her request, or rather, her demand, was properly submissive.

Dylan's gold-flecked eyes darkened to smoky amber and a soft, feral growl emanated from his throat. He spun with her in his arms and pinned her against the wall. Balancing her with one arm and the press of his body, he reached for his fly and yanked down the zipper of his black jeans. Shifting, he maneuvered until she felt the hard, perfect push of his shaft nudging its way between her legs.

There was no slow, sweet seduction. Dylan thrust into her

soaked heat, his mouth covering hers and swallowing her moans. The hot welts on her back and ass made their presence felt against the cool plaster of the wall, the erotic pain perfectly balanced with the nearly unbearable pleasure of his pounding cock.

He pressed her close with every inch of his body. Their hearts slammed against each other and found the same beat. How had she ever lived without this man? He had become a part of her, wrapped around her both in fact and in spirit. He was in her very breath, in the pulse of her blood, in the fabric of her being.

As he moved and thrust inside her, his lips traced her throat and found her collarbone. He dragged fire across her flesh, taking her to the edge of a chasm, pushing her toward it. He captured the peak of her breast with his lips. She whimpered a desperate plea. His response was fierce, his teeth and tongue on her breast tender one moment, ruthless the next.

He moved with perfect friction inside her until she was crazed with lust, mad with passion and need. When he lifted his head to kiss her mouth, she bit his lips and entwined her tongue with his, hungry for all he could give her. His smell, his taste, his very essence flooded into her and they took the leap together into a powerful, crashing orgasm that caused Dylan to sink to his knees, Zoë still wrapped around him, her body trembling.

They half-sat, half-lay against the wall in a sticky tangle of limbs. Zoë drifted in an orgasm-induced twilight, content to stay there forever, as long as Dylan continued to hold her in his arms. She finally opened her eyes when he shifted against her. He was reaching awkwardly in the front pocket of his jeans, and he produced a small, velvet box.

He pulled back and Zoë let her arms fall away. She leaned against the wall, watching him as he opened the box. Inside was a diamond ring, square-cut with dark blue sapphires on either side. Zoë sucked in her breath. She looked from the ring to Dylan's face. He was smiling, tears in his eyes. He took her left hand and held the band over her ring finger.

"Zoë Anne Stamos, I love you with all my heart. Will you marry me and be my sub girl forever?"

A laugh of pure joy bubbled its way past Zoë's lips. "Yes, Dylan Henry Hart. Yes, Sir, I will.

Available at Romance Unbound Publishing

(http://romanceunbound.com)

A Lover's Call
A Princely Gift
A Test of Love
Accidental Slave
Alternative Treatment
Beyond the Compound
Binding Discoveries
Blind Faith
Brokered Submission
Cast a Lover's Spell
Caught: Punished by Her Boss
Claiming Kelsey
Closely Held Secrets
Club de Sade
Confessions of a Submissive
Dare to Dominate
Dream Master
Face of Submission
Finding Chandler
Forced Submission
Frog
Golden Angel
Golden Boy
Golden Man
Heart of Submission
Heart Thief
Island of Temptation
Jewel Thief
Julie's Submission
Lara's Submission

Masked Submission
Obsession: Girl Abducted
Odd Man Out
Pleasure Planet
Princess
Safe in His Arms
Sarah's Awakening
Seduction of Colette
Slave Academy
Slave Castle
Slave Gamble
Slave Girl
Slave Island
Slave Jade
Sold into Slavery
Stardust
Sub for Hire
Submission in Paradise
Submission Times Two
Switch
Switching Gears
Texas Surrender
The Auction
The Compound
The Contract
The Cowboy Poet
The Inner Room
The Master
The Solitary Knights of Pelham Bay
The Story of Owen
The Toy
Tough Boy
Tracy in Chains
True Kin Vampire Tales:
Sacred Circle
Outcast
Sacred Blood

True Submission
Two Loves for Alex
Two Masters for Alex
Wicked Hearts

Connect with Claire

Website: http://clairethompson.net

Romance Unbound Publishing:
http://romanceunbound.com

Twitter: http://twitter.com/CThompsonAuthor

Facebook:
http://www.facebook.com/ClaireThompsonauthor

Blog: http://clairethompsonauthor.blogspot.com

Made in the USA
Charleston, SC
09 October 2015